RAINIER

K. LUCAS

SHADOW PRESS

A NOVEL

RAINIER

K. LUCAS

EBook ISBN: 979-8-9850093-8-5

Paperback ISBN: 979-8-9850093-9-2

Hardback ISBN: 979-8-9850093-7-8

Cover Design by Pretty In Ink Creations

Editing and Proofreading by My Brother's Editor

For my son

A NOTE FROM THE AUTHOR

This novel is a work of fiction based around the real-life Mount Rainier in Washington State. While many of the names of cities, towns, roads, etc. in this book are inspired by the real thing, they are used in a fictitious manner. Please note that this story is not meant to be accurate geographically or otherwise, and was written solely for the purpose of entertainment.

PROLOGUE

Standing in the kitchen, watching her family eat breakfast, Karen felt satisfaction wash through her. Last week, there had been a nonstop downpour of rain. It wasn't unusual for Washington, extremely common really, but it didn't stop her irritation after a week of dreary weather. Now the sun was finally shining through the morning room windows and it was the start of a perfect day.

"Pass the syrup!" her ten-year-old daughter, Melissa, called across the table.

"Where's the please?" Karen's husband, John, replied.

"Please."

"I want some too, please!" Timmy, the baby of the family at five years old, said.

Melissa drenched her pile of warm pancakes then flung the bottle of syrup at Timmy. The top wasn't on the bottle all the way, so when she threw it, syrup went everywhere. Drops of the sticky substance splashed into John's hair, across the tabletop, and a pile landed on Timmy's face.

Chaos ensued. Timmy and Melissa yelled at each other, each blaming the other, John yelled at the both of them, trying to break them apart, and Karen sighed, moving to clean up the mess between all of them. She didn't understand why the kids couldn't just enjoy a peaceful morning without bickering, but with five siblings of her own, she understood well how things naturally went.

"That's it, you two. Bedrooms, now!" John said. He tried to look stern as syrup dripped down his forehead and cheeks.

"But I didn't do anything!" Timmy cried. "She's the one who threw it!"

"I don't care. Get up there, both of you."

After the kids slumped upstairs to each of their bedrooms and Karen heard the slam of their doors, she sat down to eat her share of the pancakes before they got cold. There was a little syrup left in the bottle. She didn't have a sweet tooth anyway, so it was just enough. "You didn't have to send them upstairs," she said.

"I can't stand their damned fighting all the time." John stood by the sink, wiping himself clean.

Karen laughed. "It's part of life, dear."

"Bullshit. If I would've pulled that with my brother, my old man woulda smacked me upside the head. They're spoiled is what they are."

She heard Melissa's footsteps on the stairs but decided to stay silent. The girl would have to learn the consequences of not listening to her dad without her interference. Smiling to herself, Karen leaned back in her chair and looked out the large bay window that overlooked the hillside behind their community.

It was one of the reasons they'd bought this house. There was nothing behind them but open land, and the gorgeous view had sold her from the first time she saw it. The natural light that the window let into the house made her feel as if she were sitting outside.

Karen's smile slowly disappeared, and her brow furrowed. She was confused by what she saw outside. She started to say, "John, what's that?" but didn't have enough time to get the words out.

The enormous hill that was supposed to be there... wasn't. It had transformed into a colossal landslide that was rushing toward them at breakneck speed. By the time Karen said her husband's name, the slide had crashed into her house, swallowing it and the entire community along with it.

Thousands of tons of dirt and debris plowed into the surrounding houses, crushing everything in its wake. Houses were taken completely apart, burying the people inside under ten feet of mud, rock, and rubble. Within minutes, nothing was left. Vehicles and other large objects that were outside were carried hundreds of feet away. Most were smashed beyond recognition under the enormous weight. Anyone inside was crushed along with the metal.

The quake caused by such a large landslide alerted the nearby town of Chester. Emergency services and volunteers rushed to aid the fallen community of Rock Creek. The struggle was not just to get into the hazardous area, but to not get injured themselves by falling into the pits of mud that was like quicksand, pulling people and equipment down into its depths.

With the incident occurring on a weekend morning, more people were at home than would otherwise have been. On a weekday, many more would've been at work or otherwise out of the home. Hours passed as crews desperately searched for any survivors. They all began to lose hope as they found body after body of deceased residents and no sign of anyone living. Then, as the sun was setting, there was a call that went out.

"Over here! There's someone over here!"

A hand was reaching up through the debris, grasping air, trying to pull itself out from under a pile of siding.

"I'm here," Tina Romero cried as she reached the hand. She grasped it in hers, trying to warm the ice-cold fingers. *Jesus,* she thought, *it's so small.* Tears sprang to her eyes as she realized from the size of the hand that it could only be a child's.

"We need help over here!" Tina cried. She held the small hand in hers, waiting for others to reach their location. She knew better than to try digging the child out. If she made the wrong move, she could make things worse instead of better. The tiny fingers clasped her hand weakly, as if the child were barely awake. Tina choked back a sob. "Just hang on, baby, we're gonna get you outta there."

It didn't take long for Steve and Daniel to arrive. "It's a child," Tina whispered.

The looks on Steve and Daniel's faces were identical. They were grim but determined to help. An hour later, after digging, lifting, and sinking, the child who was buried was rescued. A cheer went out as rescuers celebrated a life saved.

"What's your name, son?" Steve asked as he helped carry the boy to the waiting ambulance.

After a coughing fit, the boy croaked, "Timmy."

"Timmy, I'm gonna hand you over to these nice people who are gonna make you feel better."

"I want my mommy."

Steve choked back tears. He didn't know what to say to this kid. How could he tell him his parents were most likely dead? "I'll try to find her for you," was the best he could manage.

Paramedics rushed Timmy to the hospital as the search and rescue team continued their efforts to find survivors. The search continued through the night and into the next several days. Even weeks later, volunteers were searching through the debris.

From his hospital room, Timmy watched the TV where the local news aired. "Five-year-old Tim Howard is the sole survivor of the Rock Creek Landslide that occurred Saturday morning around nine fifteen. He and his family lived in a two-story home, and he's suspected to have been on the upper level when the landslide occurred…"

He wasn't sure he understood everything the TV person was saying but understood that his mommy and daddy weren't there with him. He started to cry, afraid and confused. He didn't know what a landslide was. He didn't remember much other than waking up in a dark place, barely able to breathe.

A nurse walking past his room noticed him crying. She came in and changed the TV from the news to cartoons. "That's better, buddy. Let's get those tears dry now."

The nurse was right. Cartoons did help get his mind off things. He still missed his parents though. He supposed he missed Melissa too, even though she sucked most of the time.

Tim never saw his parents or sister again.

PART
ONE

CHAPTER ONE

Present Day

November was a hard time for Tim. It wasn't just that it brought back the memories of the landslide that killed his family, because it did that, but it was also the tip of the iceberg of the rainy season in Washington. With the rainy season came landslides. The memories of what happened that morning thirty years ago still plagued him, along with the determination to prevent other families from facing the same fate. They went hand in hand constantly, but *especially* with the season.

From his survival from the Rock Creek landslide, Tim grew up determined to learn about the event that wiped out his entire family and community. His interest started with a deep-rooted fear, then progressed into anger, hate, and finally simmered into a need to help others never have to face what he went through. He wanted to prevent as many children from losing their families from landslides and other natural disasters as possible.

"Tim? Are you there? Come back." The radio in Tim's Jeep went off again.

"Tim here. Headed to the summit. Over." His specialty as

a volcanologist put him front and center on volcanoes across the world, and today he was at Mount Rainier. Although his job took him all over the world, he was particularly dedicated to his home state of Washington.

"ETA on getting back to the office? Over."

"I'm not even there yet, Joe. No ETA. Over and out."

"Wait—"

Tim shut off the radio. Joe was like a naggy mother hen, always checking in on him. He knew what Tim was doing today and even though he didn't like it, he didn't have to bug him to death.

After St. Helens erupted in the eighties, equipment was stationed to constantly monitor volcano activity, not just there, but for Mount Rainier and others as well. Rainier was one that hadn't erupted in so many years, they knew an eruption was bound to happen at any time.

It wasn't a question of *if*, but *when*. The problem was, there was not enough history of eruption on record to predict the when. Tim had his own active research for Rainier. Today, he was headed up the mountain to check on his equipment.

"Welcome back, Mr. Howard," the guard at the national park gate entrance greeted when Tim flashed his badge.

Tim continued through the park, up the pass. As he traveled up the mountain, he took note of the snowmelt. There was normally snow on the mountain year round. Even in July, snow wasn't an uncommon sight. But now, in November, the sparse amount he saw was disturbing. Especially with the cool temperatures and amount of precipitation, Tim expected to see piles of fresh powder. It was there, sure, but much of it looked melted.

He felt a familiar twinge of worry when he thought about the possibility of the ground warming up. If the ground on top of a volcano was warming up, it could mean the volcano itself was warming up.

TIM SPENT HOURS AT THE SUMMIT, WORKING WITH HIS equipment, reading the data. He'd been keeping track of her for ages now and knew right off the bat when something wasn't right.

"Joe? Come back."

"Joe here. Over."

"Are you still at the office?"

Silence for a minute, and then, "What's wrong?" Joe could count on one hand the number of times Tim wanted to see him in the office. It had to be something bad.

"I'll be there in a few hours. Be there, Joe. It's urgent. Out."

Tim had checked the equipment three times. He brought back up sensors just to be safe. Everything was verified and it wasn't good. All signs were pointing to Mount Rainier waking up from her hundreds of years' hibernation. When she was fully awake, she was going to bring chaos like the country hadn't known in ages.

Tim hoped they would listen. If they didn't, it would be bad. There was more to it than just evacuating the whole west side of the state. There were politics involved. Tim knew that well enough by now.

But if they would just listen, it would mean a world of difference. He closed his eyes, envisioning the landslide that would come with the millions of pounds of snowmelt from the top of Rainier. It would be worse than anything his mind could envision. "Please let them listen," he whispered.

A T THE OFFICE , T IM SHOWED J OE THE NUMBERS . J OE SHOOK
his head. "It can't be right."

"Trust me, I made sure."

"It's just one day's worth of numbers. We need more. You know that."

"Joe, come on. With numbers like this, we need to alert someone. More people need to have their eyes on this, not just me."

Joe thought for a minute, looking back over the numbers in front of him. His forehead was starting to show droplets of sweat. This could be a career breaker if he caused panic and he was wrong.

Sure, there were people to inform, but if he spoke too soon, it would be the end of him. He would lose all credibility. He, of all people, knew it. It happened to his predecessor, after all.

"Give it a couple more days at least."

"We might not have that long, Joe. You know I've been watching her for years. I *know* this mountain."

"Oh, come on." Joe laughed. "This bitch has been asleep for so long, she's probably just stretching a little. Yes, the numbers are scary, but nothing is going to happen in a few days. Keep your mouth shut for now. That's the end of it."

T IM LEFT WITHOUT ANOTHER WORD . J OE WAS TOO WORRIED
about his own ass, and not enough about the asses of inno-

cent people who would get hurt if they called this wrong. He hated to do it, but he was going to have to go over Joe's head on this one. Joe was high on the totem pole but not top dog.

He would speak with Michelle. Surely, she would have more sense. She had a kid, if he remembered correctly. She would sympathize more with parents in the community who might be affected by this. Tim thought he would appeal to her on an emotional level if nothing else worked. If she was blind to the numbers, like Joe, he would do whatever it took. The people needed to be alerted.

CHAPTER TWO

It wasn't a far drive, but fighting traffic took Tim two hours to get to Michelle's office at the US Geological Survey Observatory in Seattle. Tim checked his watch, impatiently waiting for the elevator to lift him to the top floor of the building.

"I'm sorry, Michelle's in a meeting," her receptionist said.

"This is urgent."

"You're welcome to wait." She gestured toward an empty chair by the door.

Tim wanted to rush past her desk and barge into Michelle's office to demand an audience with her. He clenched his fists, knowing he'd get more with a sweeter treatment. He put on his most charming smile.

"I understand she's busy, but I have important data from Mount Rainier that needs to be relayed to her immediately. This is potentially life or death." His smile faded to a look of worry. "If I can't speak with her, I'll be forced to go to the media."

The receptionist picked up her phone. "She'll see you," she said, glaring at him.

A moment later, he was standing in front of Michelle's desk, waiting for her to hang up the phone. A minute passed, and then two. She had the phone to her ear but wasn't speaking. She hadn't met his eyes yet.

Tim coughed, trying to get her attention. Another minute passed. He cracked his knuckles. Finally, she looked at him.

"Sorry to cut this short, Gary," she said. "I have someone here with urgent information."

After hanging up, Michelle arched her eyebrows. "Well, Tim? Spit it out."

"Rainier is going to erupt."

She didn't look surprised.

Joe, Tim thought.

"Let's see what you have," Michelle said.

Tim passed the file to her. It was faster to have what he needed on hand, versus wasting time pulling it up on a laptop. This wasn't looking good. Joe already called her, which meant he could've said anything to downplay what was really happening.

"I assume Joe called?"

"Mm-hmm," she answered, still looking through the paperwork. Michelle finally put the papers down to look at Tim again. "This isn't the first time you've wanted to jump the gun."

"Jump the gun? Look at those numbers!" With the look she gave him, he took a calming breath. "I'm sorry. I know this is sudden, but it can't hurt anything to alert county officials. At the very least we can tell people to be ready to evacuate soon."

"And that's what I'm talking about. As soon as we mention the word 'evacuate' there's going to be hysteria. If we do that and we're wrong, we lose all credibility."

"But if we're right? I've been on Rainier for years. I know this isn't some fluke."

"Doesn't matter, and that's not the point. We need to make sure we *are* right, first."

"I *know* we are. The numbers don't lie." Tim ground his teeth together, unable to fathom why they couldn't see what he saw.

"This is from a single day?" Michelle asked.

He paused, knowing where she was going. "Like I said, I've been watching the mountain for years. I have *years* of data to compare against."

"But *these* numbers are from a single day?"

"Yes," he ground out.

"I see." She took her glasses off and placed them on top of the papers. Folding her hands together and leaning back in her chair, she assessed him. Michelle puckered her lips then sucked them in, seeming to have an internal debate. Finally, she said, "You're right to be concerned."

"But?"

"But… Joe's right. We need more than one day's worth of numbers. Give it a week."

"A week?" Tim ran his hand through his hair. "That's the protocol for numbers that are steadily climbing, yes. But this is *already* high. She could erupt tomorrow. Today, even. By next week, it could be over."

Michelle frowned. "I doubt that's going to happen."

"What about others studying Rainier? I know I'm not the only one out there who's seeing this. I can't be. Don't tell me you haven't heard from anyone else."

She shrugged. "I'm sorry, but that's exactly what I'm going to tell you. No one else has come forward with this."

Tim couldn't take any more of this. Michelle wasn't hearing him on logic, so time to try emotion. You have kids, right? "Imagine your kids at home tonight. Asleep in their beds, and the beautiful mountain they look out on decides to blow up. Think of how scared they'll be. Think of the *ash* they'll breathe."

Michelle held up a hand. "Stop. I get the point you're

trying to make. My answer is the same. Watch it for a few more days. Then I'll make the call. Put a team together if you want to, to help you collect whatever additional data you need."

Tim locked his jaw. If he said anything else, he might get fired. He couldn't believe she was so against this. He didn't need a team. He needed her to *listen*. Even putting a word in someone's ear so the *officials* were in the loop, if not the public, would be better than nothing. It would be one step closer to having some kind of preparation. At least someone out there would be prepared, which was better than the way things were right now.

Hating her stubbornness, he gave a firm nod and then turned to walk out.

"Tim?" Michelle stopped him as he had one foot through the door. "I know your history," she said. "I understand your concern. Trust the protocol. It's there for a reason."

She was trying to comfort him in her own way. Let him down a little easier, show him she wasn't holding his determination against him. Tim acknowledged it was kind of her. But he didn't want kindness. He wanted action.

He had over ten years of experience under his belt. Tim didn't need a lecture on protocol. He helped create the damned protocol. With his education and unique experience, they should be listening to him instead of shutting him down. Tim just hoped they were right. He would give anything to be wrong in a time like this, but that was rarely the case.

If it was just his gut, it would be one thing. He would leave well enough alone, but with those numbers, it was another story. He couldn't believe no other volcanologist on Rainier had said anything yet.

Tim checked the time again. Channel One News was just down the street. He could be there in a matter of minutes. As he descended back down in the elevator, he weighed the idea in his mind. His conversations with Joe and Michelle both weighed on him, creating a sliver of self-doubt. Tim *knew* he was right on this. There was no question about eruption. It was going to happen. But *when?* If he was wrong about the when, it could be just as bad as saying nothing at all.

If Tim alerted the world against his boss's instructions, and Rainier didn't erupt within a week, but then erupted a month or two down the road, when everyone already let their guard down, there would be no way to evacuate. No one would take them seriously after a false alarm. It's just like Joe and Michelle said about losing credibility. In that, *they* were right.

He sighed, hating the doubt that felt suffocating. He would give it another day. First thing in the morning, he would go back to check the numbers in person again. Recalibrate everything, triple-check, even quadruple-check if needed, until this *doubt* was gone. If the numbers were like they were today, he would go straight to the media.

If he got fired, so be it. Tim could try to remain anonymous, but his bosses would know it was him anyway. No. He wouldn't hide his face. He would show the world he was ready to stand behind his research and show how serious of a situation this was. Hopefully he could prevent all hell from breaking loose in the meantime.

CHAPTER THREE

Running on fumes from a late-night shift, Teresa guzzled her cup of coffee before setting her empty cup on the counter. If she didn't drink fast, she would get distracted with getting Luke ready for school and wind up with a cold cup. If there was enough time before drop-off, she would get herself a refill, but there usually wasn't time.

"Let's go, bud! Gonna be late!" she called from the bottom of the staircase.

"Coming!" Luke called back, peeking out his bedroom door. Today was show-and-tell day at school and he had his painted rock collection neatly organized in his box, ready to show off. He just had to turn them all facing the right way, so they were visible through the see-through top.

Last week they'd gone on a hunting mission together at three nearby parks and found rocks galore. Collecting the painted rocks was his favorite hobby and with Teresa's work schedule, it was hard for her to have the time or energy to go with him, which made these particularly special.

Luke especially loved the painted rocks with Pokémon on them. Those he always kept. The others he would hide in new places for others in the community to find. At school, there was a rock painting group that met at lunch sometimes to come up with new designs and maps on where to find hidden rocks.

They sometimes got together after school too, but it was usually the older kids that went to those meetings. Luke had just started middle school this year and Teresa didn't feel comfortable with him staying after all alone, yet.

"Luke!" Teresa called again.

Luke closed the top of his rock box and put it into his Pikachu backpack. He grinned, imagining the guys going crazy over some of his finds. He raced down the stairs and gave his mom a hug. "All ready."

THE DROP-OFF LINE WAS BACKED UP THROUGH THE SCHOOL parking lot and back out onto the street. It never failed. Every day was the same. Teresa glanced at the clock on the dash. "Do you want to walk from here? You might be late if you wait."

Luke frowned. They weren't even in the school parking lot yet. He was surprised she would ask him to walk from the sidewalk without her. He'd never done it before.

Without him saying a word, Teresa seemed to understand. "I'm sorry," she said. "Mom is just running late. Forget I asked. Let's at least get into the parking lot."

Luke breathed a sigh of relief. He didn't want to admit it, but he was a little scared to walk that far alone, especially with all the cars and people. He was glad he didn't have to look like a baby now.

Teresa was texting on her phone when a green sedan cut in front of them. She'd let the gap between them and the car in front get too wide, and the sedan took advantage. Teresa laid on the horn. "Come on, asshole!" she cried, slamming her hand on the steering wheel. The driver of the green sedan rolled down his window and held up his middle finger.

"Really nice," Teresa said. She choked back a cry. She was so tired and now running so late. Why did other parents have to be jerks in the pickup line? Everyone wanted the same thing. They all just wanted to drop their kids off safely at school and get on with their day.

"Sorry." She gave a sheepish smile to Luke.

He shrugged, used to her language, not really caring. "Just another dollar for me in the swear jar."

"I won't forget," she promised.

The line seemed to move like molasses. Creeping forward at a snail's pace, Teresa watched parents seeming to get their kids dressed in line, and others who practically threw their kids out of the car. One mom was actually standing there, doing her kid's homework, while other drivers honked for her to move out of the way.

Teresa wondered why the school didn't have a better system in place. She turned on the radio, trying to take her mind off the stress of running behind schedule. "Can you believe this guy?" a person on the radio was saying.

"I know. The nerve it takes to go behind your boss's back like that."

"Do you think his information is right?"

"If it was, why would he be the only one saying it?"

"True. Very true."

"Folks, if you're just tuning in, we're talking about a man

—a geologist—volcanologist to be specific, who's reporting that Mount Rainier is going to erupt any time. He—"

What? Teresa couldn't believe what she was hearing. She checked the radio channel to see which station she was listening to, wondering if maybe the tuner changed by accident. But it wasn't. It was her normal, everyday station. She turned the volume up, trying to get a better idea of what they were talking about.

"He says he has equipment on the volcano, taking measurements and readings. Apparently, those readings are giving him some disturbing numbers."

"More than disturbing, right? Apparently, he's convinced she's going to blow any minute."

"That's right. Now folks, we don't want to cause a panic here. And the man himself says his bosses aren't as concerned as he is—"

"Who's the man!" Teresa cried.

"Mom?" Luke asked. Teresa was too distracted, concentrating on listening to the report. Another gap had grown between her and the car in front again. The drivers behind were honking, trying to get her attention.

"Mom, scoot up," Luke said.

She looked in the rearview mirror, then back out the windshield. "Shit. Sorry." She moved the car forward in line. They were now in the parking lot, nearly to the front of the line.

"I can walk from here, now," Luke said.

"Are you sure?"

"Yeah." He nodded, grabbing his backpack.

"Sorry, Luke, you know I'm out of it today." Teresa turned around in her seat to give him a kiss.

"It's okay, Mom. I love you."

"I love you, baby."

Luke got out of the back seat and walked to class. Teresa

turned off the radio. She would research the news later if no one at work knew anything. She had to focus on driving, or she was going to get in a wreck and that was the *last* thing she could afford to do. When the car in front of her pulled forward, she had enough room to make a U-turn and get out of the parking lot without waiting on more cars.

CHAPTER FOUR

Teresa flew through traffic, desperate to clock in only eight, or even nine minutes late, instead of anything over ten. She was already on her second warning for being late. There was a ten-minute grace period for clocking in and out, and if she didn't hit the mark today, it would be bad. She suspected if her boss didn't want to date her, she would already be searching for a new job.

Teresa pulled into the first spot she found in the parking garage, then tore out of the car. As she ran to the building door, she fumbled through her purse for her badge, not paying attention to anything but her task at hand. Her fingers felt for the hard plastic, brushing past her ChapStick, gum wrappers, and spare tampon. "Where is it?" she cried.

There was no time to stop. Teresa glanced down to look inside her bag, still running. When she did, a horn blared at her. Tires screeched. The SUV hit her before she registered what was happening.

Sprawled on the ground, Teresa blinked up at the ceiling of the parking garage. Pain radiated through her spine and skull. She put a hand to her head. Then she realized she was losing minutes. As she rolled over, trying to pick up the contents of her purse that fell out, she heard a man ask, "Are you okay?"

"I'm fine."

Teresa wasn't quite steady on her feet. The man held his arm out to help steady her.

"I can't be late," she said. She finally looked at him. She felt dizzy but didn't have time to talk about it. She just needed to *clock in* then she could go on break early. Teresa gave the man a weak smile before limping the rest of the way to the door.

"You're bleeding!" the man called after her. Teresa waved her arm in the air to acknowledge she heard him.

She still hadn't found her badge. At security, the guard recognized her. "I don't know what I did with my badge," she said. "I'm so late. I don't have time for a pass. Please, I'm on my last warning." Luckily, it didn't take much begging for mercy to appeal to his sympathy.

"Don't make a habit of it, okay?" he said.

"You're a lifesaver. You have no idea!" she called when he buzzed her through.

She sat down at her desk, clocking in and putting her headset on at exactly eight forty.

"You're late."

Go away! Teresa screamed in her head. "Hi Jerry," she said aloud. She turned around to face him, letting him see the blood still dripping down her forehead.

"Shit, what happened?" he asked.

"Got hit by a car." Teresa heard a beep through her headset. "Sorry, Jerry, got to take this."

"We'll talk later," he said, walking away.

"This is 9-1-1, what is your emergency?" Teresa said, answering the call.

By lunchtime, eighty percent of the calls Teresa had taken were callers concerned with the longtime silent volcano erupting. She'd had to talk countless people out of their panic.

So many of them demanded to see a police officer, which didn't make sense to her. What was a police officer supposed to do for them? With the current police shortage, there was no way to send officers out to every single person that wanted to *talk* about Mount Rainier erupting.

Ordinarily, Teresa would avoid speaking to Jerry like the plague, but today she needed some answers. There had been no communication about talking points regarding the eruption, and no communication about the eruption at all, for that matter. She was working off the basis that it was false information because she had nothing else to go by, other than what she'd heard on the radio.

As she swiped her card at the vending machine while on break, she noticed a coworker standing a few feet away getting coffee. "Have all your calls been about Rainier, too?" Teresa asked.

"Yup. Almost all of them."

"What have you been telling them?"

"The usual, please remain calm, the mountain isn't going to explode, we haven't been informed of anything at this time but if you're afraid for your life, safely evacuate."

"Same here. Jerry hasn't said anything?"

She laughed. "Yeah, right."

Jerry walked into the break room. *Speak of the devil,* Teresa thought. She walked to meet him. "Jerry, are there talking points on the situation with Mount Rainier?"

"What about Mount Rainier?" He looked at her like she was crazy.

"All the calls coming in today are people worried about it erupting. You haven't heard?"

"Completely unfounded. I haven't heard a thing."

Teresa couldn't believe how uninformed Jerry was. It wasn't just this incident, either. This happened all the time, where she or another dispatcher would have to fill him in on current events. It was crazy how he was still in charge. Although she had to admit, if not for the radio earlier, she would be just as clueless as Jerry right now.

"On the radio this morning, someone from the US Geological Survey was saying he had significant evidence—"

"Oh that!" Jerry barked. He started laughing. "People are taking that seriously?"

Teresa's brow furrowed. "Yes… of course they are. Are you kidding?"

He sobered. "There's been no *official* announcement. Treat it as hearsay until otherwise notified."

Teresa nodded. She turned, but Jerry added, "We need to speak about your tardiness."

"I told you I was hit by a car. I was within my ten-minute leeway."

"You're walking a fine line here, Teresa."

"I'll tell that to the next guy that wants to hit me with his SUV."

"Are you okay?"

She couldn't tell if it was real concern in his eyes or not. "Just a headache. Thanks." Teresa held up her snack, then left him to eat. After all the chatting, she only had five minutes left to eat before putting her headset back on. She stuffed her face as fast as she could while searching for any information she could find on Rainier. She went to the radio station's website to see if they had information. When nothing came up, she did a Google search, where Channel One News came up. There was an interview early that morning with a geologist named Tim Howard.

Teresa searched the US Geological Survey website. "The interview on Channel One News this morning featured a former employee. The individual was speaking without all the facts, and we apologize for the misinformation provided. We are keeping a close eye on Mount Rainier at this time, however, there is no indication of an imminent eruption. Please remain calm and disregard the premature warning that was issued earlier today." The headline was in bold across the top of the web page. *Tim sure pissed someone off,* she thought.

They wanted everyone to forget about it and go back to their normal lives. It was understandable, given the amount of worry the interview had already caused. But something didn't sit right with her. They were trying to shut him up, instead of telling people the facts that he *did* have. Why wouldn't they just say he read the numbers wrong or something? They called it a *"premature warning."* What did that mean?

CHAPTER FIVE

Jordan took a deep breath before ringing the doorbell to his parents' new apartment. His mother and father had just moved into a one-bedroom apartment in a senior-living complex, and he couldn't let go of the guilt he felt for letting them live in a place like this.

It wasn't that it was bad living conditions, in fact, they had a really nice apartment. It was small, yes, but still cozy and even had its own fireplace, washer and dryer, and granite counters. The guilt he felt was more that *he* should be taking care of them and couldn't.

He wanted to be someone successful so he could afford a nice home that would have plenty of room for them. If he made more money, he could be a son that they relied on. One who took care of his elderly parents. That was something easier said than done, though.

Jordan saw the disappointment in his father's eyes any time he mentioned work. Working at a gas station didn't earn as much as a doctor, didn't Jordan know? Jordan saw the embarrassment on his father's face, unable to stand the fact that his son was a nobody.

"Not everyone can be a doctor, Dad," he'd said after dropping out of college. "Not everyone *wants* to be one."

"Think of your responsibility, not what you want, son," his father had said.

"I have a responsibility to myself, too."

"You must decide which of your responsibilities is the most important. Sometimes we make sacrifices in life for the greater good."

It was fifteen years ago that he'd dropped out to live life the way he wanted. He spent years *living*, not regretting his choice, until recently. Watching his parents grow old before his eyes was hard. His father, so strong, so stern, now hunched with old age. They'd had Jordan later in life, when his mother was nearly forty-five and his father even older. They'd had another son who died in an accident years prior.

The story of his deceased brother only served to add to the guilt now that he was older and his brother hadn't survived past childhood. Jordan couldn't help but wonder if his brother had lived what he would be like. Would he be a man capable of taking care of his parents? There was no doubt in his mind that it was what his father thought.

Picking up extra shifts any time the opportunity arose, Jordan was working nearly sixty hours every week now that the guilt was eating away at him. He had almost no social life because going out cost money. Money he could be saving to help his parents. He reminded himself no matter what his situation was, they had it worse. Neither was physically able to work any longer, and both relied on meager social security checks for survival.

Jordan choked back the guilt every time he saw his parents. He wanted to avoid them but didn't know if the guilt of abandoning them would be worse than the guilt of not being able to take care of them. Besides, he would miss his mother too much. Unlike his father, she looked at him with nothing but love in her eyes, no matter Jordan's financial situation.

"Jordy!" his mother greeted him, hugging him tightly before ushering him through the apartment door.

"Hi Mom," Jordan said as the dog yipped at his feet. "Hi Chong boy." He laughed as his parents' little chihuahua licked his hand. Jordan looked around the apartment, noticing how many full boxes were still piled against the walls. "Need some help unpacking?" They'd been moved in for over a month now, but from the number of unpacked boxes, it seemed like it had only been a week.

"Oh, no, no, we're fine. We just like to go slow. Are you hungry?"

Jordan smelled the soup his mother had on the stove. His mouth watered as the aroma of it wafted to his nose. "Starving. Thanks, Mom." He walked to the empty chair in the living room, next to the one his dad was sitting in. "Hi Dad."

"Jordan," his father said, not looking up from his tablet.

Jordan pulled Chong up into his lap to scratch his belly. The familiar feeling of awkwardness enveloped him as he waited for his mother to bring him his bowl of soup. He racked his brain for something to say, coming up with nothing. He didn't think anything he wanted to talk about would ever be of interest to his father.

"Did you hear about Mount Rainier?" his father surprised Jordan by asking.

"Mount Rainier? No. What happened?"

"They're saying it's going to erupt."

"What? When?"

"Soon."

Jordan's eyes bulged. "We have to get you guys out of here. What are we doing? We need to go." Jordan set Chong back on the floor before standing up. He looked at his father expectantly, but he remained sitting, not even glancing in Jordan's direction.

"Dad? Why aren't we going? This is serious."

"Nonsense. Even if it does erupt, we're too far away to care."

"But Dad, what about breathing the ash? What if something goes wrong?" He wanted to say, "You guys are too old to move fast in a hurry." But caught himself. He didn't think his father would want to hear that.

"If something goes wrong? What can go wrong? It's a volcano. It shoots out lava then it goes back to sleep."

Jordan was amazed at his father's ignorance. He wasn't afraid at all, not even concerned. He wondered why he brought up the topic at all if he wasn't willing to evacuate. Jordan looked to his mother. "Mom, aren't you worried?" When she met his gaze, he could tell that she was.

"Your father thinks we'll be fine."

"Mom, come with me," he whispered. "We can leave now while there's not a panic."

She shook her head. "No, son. I can't leave your father." She took a step closer to whisper, "It reminds him too much of when we lost your brother."

Of course. Jordan grew up on the stories of what happened to his brother. The accident that took him from their family. "But this is nothing like that," he whispered back.

She shrugged her shoulders, saying nothing else.

Jordan clenched his fists. Why were his parents being so stubborn? More importantly, how did his dad hear this news and he hadn't? Wasn't the volcano erupting something of high importance? Shouldn't there be an emergency broadcast to alert everyone?

"Dad," Jordan said. "Where did you hear this information?"

"There was an interview on the news earlier today."

After inhaling his soup, Jordan spent time talking with his mom and doing research on his phone. He wanted to find out exactly what was going on, since his dad was being vague, and no amount of cajoling would convince either of his parents to leave.

He thought about getting them to leave under the guise of going out to eat. Maybe he could offer to buy them some lunch, just to get them in the car. From there, they would be safe. But they'd have no belongings. And what about Chong? His mother would be heartbroken if she had to leave her little dog behind.

"Hey, do you guys want to go grab some lunch?"

"The soup wasn't enough? Do you want another bowl, son?" his mother asked.

Jordan felt like an idiot. *Of course, the soup*, he thought. "No, no it was fine, Mom. I meant another day. Can I take you out to lunch tomorrow?"

"That would be nice, thank you," she said, smiling.

Jordan glanced at his father, who was still staring at his tablet. "How do you feel about going for a drive today?" Jordan asked. "We can go to Gig Harbor or something. Or what about the ferry over to Vashon Island? Mom loves the ferry, right, Mom?"

"Oh, that sounds fun!" his mother said. "Quan, what do you think?"

Hope lurched in Jordan's chest. If she could convince his father to go, they'd be saved. Even if the volcano wasn't going to erupt for a week or two, they'd be safe, out of the state.

He'd use his credit card to get them a hotel room somewhere. The rest would take care of itself. There had to be a reason this geologist was saying what he was saying. If he had the numbers to show it, if he felt it so strongly that he was willing to go behind his boss's back to say it, Jordan believed there had to be some truth to it.

QUAN LOOKED INTO HIS WIFE'S EYES. HIS FEATURES SOFTENED when he saw her excitement. The two of them didn't go to very many places without Jordan because it was hard for him to drive. His reflexes weren't what they once were. After moving, he'd been feeling weaker than ever, not that he'd admit it to his son.

"Sure," he said.

"Great!" Jordan said. He scooped up Chong. "Let's go."

"What are you doing with Chong?"

"He can come too, can't he?"

"Why would you want to bring him?" Quan arched an eyebrow.

"I just thought Mom would like to. Mom?" Jordan turned to his mother, silently pleading for her to understand.

She shrugged. "I don't care. We can leave him here if you want to."

"Leave him. I don't want to deal with letting him do his business."

Jordan swallowed the lump in his throat. Setting Chong back down, he wondered if his mom was ever going to forgive him.

CHAPTER SIX

Charlotte walked into the living room, where her husband was *still* watching the news. Really, he was lying back in the easy chair, hands folded over his gut, snoring, while the news played in the background. The volume on the television was so loud it was making her head ache.

The old man was half-deaf and refused to go in and get a hearing aid. "I don't need one of those things," he'd said when she urged him. Instead, he just turned the volume up louder.

Charlotte thought it was funny how Jim always fell asleep while watching the damned Channel One News. He *had* to watch it daily. He was almost religious about it. And every time she walked into the room, he was asleep with it playing in the background.

She couldn't stomach the daily news herself. Current events were always too depressing, and with the way Jim passed out while watching every day, she thought there had to be something really boring about them too.

"Jim!" Charlotte called. "Wake the hell up!" She had to yell just to hear herself over the television. Charlotte went to the back of Jim's chair and pushed it down hard, startling him awake. His headrest almost touched the floor with her effort. Jim choked on a snore and threw his hands out to his sides to steady himself.

"Good God, woman! Are you tryin' to kill me?"

Charlotte couldn't help but laugh at his reaction. Watching the old man flop around in his chair like a fish out of water was the funniest thing she'd seen in ages. "I'm sorry," she said, wiping tears from her cheeks. "Turn off the TV, would ya? You have it up so damned loud."

Jim gave her a look that would melt ice. He reached for the remote to turn the volume down. "They were talking about Rainier earlier. I wanted to see if they had anything else to say about it."

"Something good enough to make you fall asleep? Wow, can't wait to hear about it."

"Do you always have to be like that?"

"What?"

"So goddamned negative!" Jim cried.

"I'm not being negative. It's the truth! You were sitting there snoring two seconds ago." Charlotte couldn't understand what he was having a fit about. He was sure getting cranky in his old age.

Jim wasn't in the mood to hear his wife's bickering. He turned the volume back up on the television, even louder than it was before. With a huff, Charlotte left the room. The back door slammed behind her as she went to sit on the back patio.

Living in Orting, the couple were fortunate to own a house with a breathtaking view of the mountain. When they'd bought the house, Charlotte didn't even have to see inside to know she wanted it. The back porch was where she swore she'd be most of the time, and for thirty years it had been.

"Hey, old girl. They're talking about you on the telly, I guess," Charlotte said. Talking to the mountain was something she did often. It was therapeutic in a way, and she didn't see what it would hurt if she treated her mountain as an old friend.

With a cloudless sky, the mountain was out today, in full view. A rare sight for the rainy season. Charlotte leaned back on her porch swing, taking in the majestic view. The muffled sounds of Jim's television inside relaxed her now that it wasn't blaring in her ears. She closed her eyes, swinging back and forth slowly, steadily, until she was the one snoring.

Inside, Jim was trying to decide if the man on the news was full of shit or really knew what he was talking about.

"Mount Rainier is considered an active volcano, yes, and it wouldn't be unusual for some of our data to suggest movement. It's being closely watched, of course, just like any active volcano."

There was something about the man's face that Jim didn't like. Some geologist. He was a different guy than they had earlier, and he was smooth. A little too smooth for Jim's taste.

"Should residents be worried about tremors or any lava flow?" the news anchor asked.

"Tremors aren't uncommon. They happen all the time, in fact, and are usually so small that they're unnoticeable. With increased activity, yes, some small tremors might become more noticeable, especially now that everyone's mind is on it." He smiled. "But no, people should not be concerned about lava flow. We are not concerned with Mount Rainier erupting at this time."

"Thanks, Joe. I'm sure everyone will breathe a little easier now." The news anchor turned to a different camera. "Ladies and gentlemen, that was Joe Gibson of the US Geological Survey."

"Uh-huh," Jim said. His brows furrowed the longer he

watched. The more they spit out, the more worried he became. Jim thought it would be different if they had the same guy on from earlier in the day, but he'd disappeared. Why were they trying to shut the guy up? If he was a nobody, they wouldn't have interviewed him in the first place.

A helicopter flew overhead, followed by a second and then a third. The rapid succession, at a low altitude, was ear-splitting to Charlotte, still asleep on the swing out back. She startled awake and when she opened her eyes, her throat caught. "Jim!" she cried. "Jim, you better come out here!" Her mountain. Her beautiful mountain was letting out dark-gray smoke.

Jim fought to get out of his chair. He leaned forward, didn't quite make it, then leaned back again. With the momentum of the chair, he swung forward, finally able to pull himself up and out of his seat. His bones cracked as he stretched his back.

Normally he wouldn't make the effort to get up, but with all this bullarky going on today, he thought it might be worth the effort. He made his way to the back door to see what all the fuss was about. "What is it?" he asked.

On the porch, his eyes grew wide. "Holy Mary." Jim grabbed his wife's hand, holding it firmly in his. "I think it's time we pack," he said, watching the smoke billowing out of the top of the mountain.

CHAPTER SEVEN

Tim had been unable to resist. Logic told him he was a fool for trying to go behind Joe's and Michelle's backs but his emotions and sense of what was right and what was wrong won out. How could he look at cold, hard facts and pretend to ignore them? Rainier was going to erupt. It was that simple.

After checking his numbers again, recalibrating his equipment, and making damn sure he wasn't wrong, he'd called his contact at Channel One. "Kelly, I need an interview this morning. It's important."

They'd been all too willing to air the story. And, when Joe fired him, they'd been all too willing to turn on him and talk about the havoc a disgruntled employee can wreak. Joe was up in arms the minute the interview was over.

"Are you insane?" he cried.

"No, Joe, just trying to save people's lives."

"You're going to cause chaos, is what you're going to do! You're not going to save anyone. In fact, you're probably going to make it worse."

"Joe, people need to be prepared. They need to be warned."

"We talked about this already and you went deliberately

behind my back. You tried going to Michelle too, I heard. And now this. You're fired, Tim."

"Joe—"

"I'm sorry. I have to go." Joe hung up then, not giving Tim a chance to explain his actions any further. Tim had known there was a chance it would happen, and yet somehow he was still surprised. He'd worked with Joe for years. They'd been through a lot together, including actual volcanic eruptions. Joe knew well what would happen if half the state of Washington panicked at the same time.

The eruption was just part of it. The worst wouldn't be the tremors or the lava or the ash. It wouldn't even be the landslides. The worst part of it all would be the panic. If it came out of nowhere, they weren't ready, had no idea it was going to happen, it would be utter chaos.

People would literally trample each other in the streets. They would loot. They would *kill*. All because they were panicked. They would be afraid for their lives. They'd have every right to be terrified; a volcanic eruption was one of the most terrifying things a person could encounter, but it was a matter of trying to prevent the *panic*.

Tim had been in Seattle when Joe's call came through. From there, there was only one thing left to do. The people in the immediate vicinity of the mountain were going to be the worst off. He had to at least try warning those at the national park.

"I NEED TO SPEAK WITH SOMEONE IN CHARGE," JOE SAID AT THE Mount Rainier ranger station. He flashed his badge, as always, hoping they wouldn't question his presence.

"We got a call in this morning from someone at the US Geological Survey in Seattle. They warned us you would be coming by," one of the rangers said.

Tim felt his face flush. *Damn.* He'd been hoping to stay one step ahead of Joe, but it seemed Joe had caught on. "Great," Tim said, hoping he'd be able to still get through to them. If they shut him out, he didn't know what he would do. "Did they tell you the urgent news?" he asked. His face radiated concern that was real.

The ranger's brow furrowed. "I'm not sure. Let me get my boss."

Thank God, Tim thought as he waited to speak with someone who could help evacuate the park. As minutes passed, he started to pace. The time on his watch read 2:10. He wondered how he was going to convince this person to evacuate the park when he had no official backing.

"Can I help you?" another park ranger greeted.

"Yes, I'm with the US Geological Survey. I have urgent news about Rainier. It's vital that we evacuate the park as soon as possible. Immediately, in fact."

The ranger's eyes went wide. "On what grounds?"

"On what grounds?" Tim barked a laugh. "On the grounds that my data reads she's on the verge of exploding any day, any time."

She looked doubtful. "There's been no signs to suggest something like that happening. There's been no steam, no tremors, nothing. Everything has been completely normal."

Tim scoffed. "Normal? It's normal for Rainier to act up a little now and again. Her being completely silent is *not* normal."

The ranger blushed. "Well, you know what I mean. There's nothing going on to suggest to the average person that there's going to be an eruption."

"That may be. But the numbers don't lie. And I'm not an

average person. I have equipment that is *designed* to monitor an active volcano. Trust me when I say I am not lying. This is not a false alarm."

She pursed her lips, contemplating. Tim clenched his fists, trying to maintain control of his temper. *What was there to think about here?* he thought. The ranger began to shake her head back and forth. "I'm not sure I have the authority to evacuate the park. I'll have to make a call."

"Of course you have the authority. This is an emergency!" Tim yelled.

It was a mistake to lose control. The ranger frowned now, distrust in her eyes. "I'll have to make some phone calls. I'm sure you understand if I need to verify the information you're giving me."

Tim sighed. "Go ahead."

When she went back into her office, presumably to call Joe, Tim left. There was nothing else for it. He would have to go up to everyone he saw and warn them himself. He would look like a crazy person, but if he could help just a handful of people, it would be better than no one at all.

"Please, you have to listen to me. The mountain is going to erupt! You have to get your family and get the hell out of here as fast as you can," Tim said.

"What?" The man Tim was speaking with had on hiking gear. He and his family were crossing the road, headed to a trail. They were the first ones Tim came across to warn.

"The volcano is going to erupt," Tim said. He wanted to scream it at this man, who was staring at him in confusion, but he had a feeling if he yelled, he would sound even crazier, and the man wouldn't listen at all.

"I don't understand. What volcano?" the man asked.

Tim ground his teeth together, fighting his temper back. "Mount Rainier is an active volcano. I'm a geologist and I've been doing research on the summit. This volcano is going to erupt. You need to evacuate immediately."

The words finally seemed to get through to the man. His mouth gaped open as the severity of Tim's words hit home. "Holy shit!" the man cried. He herded his family back the way they'd come. *One down, how many to go?* Tim thought.

He got back into his Jeep with the intention of going to the visitor center. There would be people there for sure. It was a good place to start. As Tim was driving, he noticed the trees starting to sway violently out the window. He stopped the car. As he did, he felt the steering wheel trembling. Vibrating was coming up through the ground, shaking his vehicle.

Oh, no, Tim thought. The sound of the rumbling was so distinct, Tim thought she was going to spew lava right then. He floored the accelerator, desperate to reach the visitor center. It wasn't at the summit, but it was high enough up, where anyone who was there would probably be killed from debris, if not the lava.

CHAPTER EIGHT

At the visitor center, Tim was surprised to find only a handful of people. Normally there would be more, so it was a relief to find so few. Another tremor hit, shaking the building and those inside. The panicked looks on everyone's faces had Tim sweating with worry. He had to tell them to evacuate, but if he yelled, "The volcano is going to erupt!" he thought it would ignite the panic that he'd wanted to prevent.

Tim hoped the tremors would be enough to get people to leave on their own. "Ladies and gentlemen," he called when the shaking stopped. "I'm with the US Geological Survey, and I'd like to ask everyone to please calmly head back to your vehicles now. The park is closing early today."

Some looked confused, some looked worried, but everyone seemed to have a hint of relief on their faces. No one wanted to look like a coward and head for the door first. It was easier if the decision to go was made for them.

"What's going on?" someone called.

"The volcano is having some tremors," Tim said. "It's safer for everyone to leave the park."

"Will we get a refund?" several asked as they passed.

Tim made his way to the second floor, where he informed

anyone who wasn't already headed downstairs. The employees were worried too. They didn't question his authority.

"Is it going to erupt?" a kid asked as he passed Tim. No one else was around at this point. Everyone had already made their way·to the front door or outside to the parking lot.

"Most likely, yes," Tim said. He looked around for an adult who might be with the kid. "Where're your parents?"

"That's so *cool!* I want to stay and watch!" the kid cried.

"Hey, no, kid. Trust me, this is *not* cool. It's dangerous. Where're your parents?" Tim asked again.

"At work." The kid started to wander off, heading for the enormous glass windows overlooking the mountain and parking lot below. Tim could see a hiking trail that led to the summit. There were people coming down it, headed toward the parked cars.

"Who are you here with then?" Tim called, running after him. "We have to get out of here."

"I'm with my class. We're on a field trip. The others went hiking but I have a sprained ankle and so they left me here to hang out until they get back."

"They did *what?*" Tim was furious for this kid. How could any adult leave a kid behind like that? It was heartless. Weren't schools supposed to make sure everyone stayed with the group, no matter what?

Tim thought in his day something like this would've never happened. At least he hoped it wouldn't have. He clenched his fists. If he was this kid's dad, he would let his fury rain down on that school and teacher, or whoever was in charge. Tim closed his eyes and took a deep breath, not wanting to scare the kid. When he opened them, the kid was gone.

"Kid? Hey, kid, where'd you go?" Tim started to panic. He

and the kid were the last ones in the building as far as he knew. They had to get the hell out of there and quick. Tremors could mean anything. They could mean nothing, and they could mean she was about to blow. There was no way for him to know and he wasn't about to take any chances. That was the whole point of his trip there today.

"I'm over here," the kid called, peeking out of the gift shop.

When Tim reached him, the kid was putting a souvenir pocketknife into his backpack. He shrugged. "My parents didn't send any money with me."

Tim didn't want to get into a lecture with this kid about right and wrong. The kid wasn't his problem, but he had to get him out of there. "Kid, I don't care what you do. We've got to get the hell out of here though. No more chitchat." Tim grabbed the kid's arm and started pulling him toward the staircase.

"Hey, go slower! My ankle!" The kid struggled to keep up with Tim's long stride.

"Sorry, we have to hurry."

Once outside, Tim felt panic fill his veins all over again. His breath caught in his throat as he looked up to see the smoke filling the air. They were running out of time.

He started to jog, pulling the kid along with him. "I can't go that fast," the kid huffed.

"No choice, kid," Tim called.

They reached his Jeep, and he didn't have to tell the kid to climb in. He would deal with finding his parents later. Tim chirped the tires as he drove them back down toward the park entrance. Where it had seemed like there was nobody at the park before, now that everyone was leaving at the same time, the road was congested.

Someone ahead was driving at a snail's pace, forcing traffic behind to stop and go every few seconds. Horns were blaring as impatient drivers, desperate to get out, yelled in frustration out their windows.

The elderly woman in the front of the line didn't seem to notice. She held her camera out the window, taking pictures of the waterfalls and deer crossing the road. "Get out of the fucking way!" someone yelled.

"Come on! We're all gonna die here, lady!" another shouted.

The woman didn't seem to understand the urgency and why everyone was trying to leave at once. A few cars flew past her on the other side of the road. Tim was about to do the same, just so he could let her know what was happening. Finally, a ranger pulled alongside her car.

They were almost to the gate. Tim could see it from where they were. He clenched the steering wheel in both fists, silently praying the mountain would give them enough time.

The ranger speaking with the elderly woman didn't pull her over to the side of the road so others could pass. Instead, he stopped her right where she was, now blocking both lanes of traffic. He was out of his truck, speaking to the woman through her window. There was no way around.

While he waited, Tim used his radio to try calling Joe. "Joe, come back." He waited but there was only static. With a huff, Tim pulled out his phone. It rang four times and he thought for sure Joe would ignore the call, but he answered. "Joe! I'm at Rainier and it's going to blow. Tremors, now smoke. Do you still doubt me? Do you need more evidence than this?"

Silence on the line.

"Joe?"

"There's still not enough to suggest it's going to happen immediately."

"Are you kidding me? How many years have you been a

geologist? You know *exactly* how it goes down. Don't let your pride get in the way, goddammit!"

"I'll call Michelle."

"You don't need to call Michelle! You need to call the media. Tell them you were wrong about everything. Tell people they need to evacuate safely so no one gets hurt."

"I'll take care of it."

"Hurry up about it. There's not much time left."

As Tim and the kid continued to wait for the woman and the ranger to move their vehicles out of the road so everyone else could pass, the kid sitting next to him said, "My name is Nate. In case you were wondering." He looked out the window as he spoke.

Tim felt a twinge of guilt in his gut. The kid was probably scared and from the looks of him, lonely as hell. What would it feel like to have your entire class leave you behind? He hadn't exactly been nice to the kid, either. "Nice to meet you, Nate. I'm Tim."

CHAPTER NINE

Nate turned from the window to look at Tim. He smiled. "It's—"

Another tremor rocked them. Through the windshield, they watched the ranger cabin at the entrance shake until it collapsed. The park gates tore off the railing, falling to block the road.

The line of cars in front of them were all rocking violently on the road, some of the smaller ones even bounced so their wheels completely left the asphalt.

When the shaking stopped, the sound of people's screams filled the air. Tim could only imagine how the rest of the state was going to react. He wondered how far the tremors could be felt. Probably not any large cities, but he was sure this last one probably went all the way to Elbe.

Babies were crying, men and women were yelling at each other, horns continued to blare. The elderly woman speaking with the park ranger was so startled, she floored the gas pedal, lurching her car forward. The ranger was standing too close. When her car heaved forward without warning, he didn't have time to move his foot out of her tire's path.

"Ahhh!" he wailed in agony as the bones in his foot were crushed beneath the weight of her car.

The woman didn't notice and didn't look back. Her car flew into the front gate that had fallen across the road. Her front end smooshed like an accordion, but it moved the gate enough for other cars to follow behind her.

Smoke was now not only billowing out of Mount Rainier, but from the woman's car too. The line of traffic that had been waiting for her to finally move, now had the chance to go around.

Car after car passed the injured park ranger without stopping. Tim thought about stopping to help. He thought about how much time they might have left. If the volcano erupted, they were so close they would get caught in the blast.

Then he thought about the panic. He thought about how people were *already* panicking and there had only been some tremors and smoke. Shit was going to hit the fan. Someone had to set an example. Someone had to remind people how to behave like human beings.

Tim went to pull his Jeep to the side but the car in front of him stopped first, surprising him. "Thank God," Tim muttered under his breath. The man who stopped waved at Tim to continue on without them.

Tim rolled down his window as he and Nate passed. "Are you sure?" Tim asked.

"I'm a doctor," the man said. "We'll be okay. Thanks."

"If you can, take him with you out of here and have a look once you've reached Elbe. You want to be out of the blast zone as soon as possible."

The doctor's eyes went wide with surprise. He didn't argue, just gave a firm nod of acknowledgment.

"Do you need help getting him in the car?" The doctor was already moving to help the man into the back seat of his car. One of the kids in back had moved over to make room.

"Go on, get out of here," the doctor said. He had the injured ranger in hand, yelling at Tim over the man's cries.

Tim didn't like to leave them alone without help, but if he was a doctor and said he had the situation in hand, he wasn't about to argue. He had enough people trying to argue with him when he had things in hand and knew all too well how frustrating it could be.

Five minutes later, Tim and Nate were in Ashford. Outside, they saw people rushing around in their yards, loading up cars and setting animals free. One man was sitting in his front yard with a cardboard sign that read "The end is here. Embrace it."

At one house, a woman was in tears, chasing her children around the yard, trying to get them inside the car. "Get over here!" she was screaming at them.

Tim looked over at Nate. "You might want to close your eyes as we go through town. It's only going to get worse."

"Why are people acting so crazy?"

"They're scared. People do crazy things when they're afraid."

Ashford was a tiny town, barely a blip on the map, but now it seemed the entire population was either packing in their driveways or on the road, headed toward Elbe.

Tim wondered about the other side of Rainier. The north side, and the other entrances to the national park. He hoped everyone had been able to get out. He hoped Joe had been able to make whatever call he needed to make.

They'd slowed to a crawl now that everyone was on the road. "Why don't you drive on that side?" Nate asked, pointing to the opposite side of the double yellow line. No cars were traveling in that direction, and none were utilizing it to move forward either.

Everyone should've been using that side. Nate was right. In fact, it was part of the official evacuation plan, to have the opposite side of the highway changed so that all traffic flowed in the same direction.

Since there was no organization at this point, no one knew. "You're right. Hang on," Tim said. He turned the steering wheel and pulled forward to the opposite side of the road. He rolled down his window to wave at the cars behind, hoping they'd catch on and follow.

Two minutes later, it sounded like a bomb went off. The sound of the explosion filled the air and Tim knew what was coming. "Hang on!" he yelled. He slammed on the brakes and tucked his and Nate's head down.

The roar of the blast was deafening. It was as if the earth itself was screaming through a funnel, spitting fire. Moments later, rocks pounded down all around, the sound of shattering glass and car roofs caving in seemingly endless.

A stampede of forest animals rushed past. People were screaming louder than ever. Those in their yards were dropping like flies, being hit by the flying debris, or trampled by wild animals.

"Oh my God," Nate yelled, peeking out the window.

"Get back down!"

"Those people are on *fire*!"

Tim grimaced. "Don't look at it, kid! Don't look!" He pushed Nate back down and covered him with his body. There was still a chance they could share the same fate as the others.

He thought about driving but there was no way he could navigate through this. Not with people running everywhere, other cars running all over everything, and the animals stampeding through it all. He'd wreck his Jeep before they got a mile down the road.

"Just hang tight," Tim said. "As soon as we can get out of here, we will. I promise."

PART
TWO

CHAPTER TEN

A few hours into her shift, Teresa was ready for it to be over. Her job was normally high stress, but she still loved it. It was exciting and she got to help people who were often in the worst situations of their lives.

Today had been different than normal. Different because of Rainier. She couldn't stop worrying about Luke. She wanted to leave so she could go get him from school and they could evacuate. Teresa had some sick leave saved up that she could use if necessary.

The problem was, she wasn't entirely sure yet that it was the right move. Jerry kept hovering around her like a hawk, waiting for her to screw up. "Yes ma'am, I'm sure." Teresa was saying to the woman on the line.

"I don't understand how you can say that, though. I can see the steam coming out the top right now, with my own eyes."

Teresa looked around, wondering if others were getting the same calls coming in. How could she keep telling people to disregard the idea of a volcanic eruption? "There have been no alerts from the US Geological Survey. Their official response is that it is *not* about to erupt. If you have further questions, you can contact them. This is an emergency number, ma'am. Do you have a life-or-death emergency?"

She tried to keep the irritation out of her voice, but it was hard. People called emergency services but didn't understand what the word "emergency" meant. Although, she had to give them a little credit on this one.

Teresa's hands started shaking. She held them up to her face then looked around. It wasn't *her* that was shaking. It was the whole building. The lights flickered.

"Are you still there?" the woman asked through her head-set. She'd been droning on, trying to argue.

"Ma'am, if you are not afraid for your life at the moment, I'm going to disconnect the call."

"No! Wait!"

"Are you in immediate, life-threatening danger?"

"No. But—"

"Please call the nonemergency line then. Goodbye." Teresa disconnected the call and unplugged her headset, noticing others around her doing the same.

"Was that an earthquake?" someone asked.

"I think it was Rainier," another said.

Rainier, Teresa thought. Then she thought about her son. All hell was going to break loose if it was the volcano. As a dispatcher, it was her job to man the phones when disaster struck. There were mandatory overtime requirements in place for events like this. Nobody was able to leave.

How could she *not?* It would be all Jerry needed to pull the plug on her. Did she risk leaving, even not knowing anything that was happening? If she got fired over this, how would she support Luke when it was all over?

Teresa clenched her jaw, wishing she would've acted sooner. She got up from her desk, cell phone in hand.

"What do you think you're doing?" Jerry asked, startling her.

"God, Jerry, do you have to be there every time I stand up? You scared the crap out of me."

Jerry smiled. "Just keeping an eye on one of my best employees. Where are you going?"

Teresa threw up her hands. "Did you not just see what happened?"

"Exactly. We need all hands on deck right now. Plug that headset back in."

"I need to make a personal call. I'm worried about my son."

He huffed. "Five minutes, then back to it."

"Thanks, Jerry." Teresa smiled at him, holding her attitude back as much as she could. He was being an ass, but she couldn't hold it against him too much. That's just the way he was. He was also her boss, and she didn't have much choice other than to deal with him.

There were others who had the same idea as Teresa. Many sat at their desk texting or making personal calls, checking on loved ones. Teresa walked to a hallway near the bathroom where it was quieter. She made the call to her son's school, but the phone line gave the busy tone. Teresa hung up, wanting to cry.

She was so torn on what to do. Did she risk her career or not? She thought for a moment, wondering what else she could do. Teresa wondered if she was the worst mother on the planet, putting her career before her son. Then she told herself having a career *was* for her son. She told herself that others were going to need her help too, and it was her job to be there for them, *especially* in a time like this.

Teresa was determined to make sure Luke was safe no matter what. Even if she had to stay put, she could do something to ensure his safety. They didn't have anyone in their lives they could count on. There was no father figure for Luke, no extended family, it was just the two of them.

She racked her brain, trying to think of a way to reach her son. Then she remembered Luke's best friend's mom, Naomi. With the boys' relationship they'd become more than just mom acquaintances. They weren't quite friends because Teresa was too busy to invest time into a friendship of any kind, but thought if she did have the time, Naomi could be a good friend.

Naomi answered after the first ring. "Teresa, thank God, do you have any idea what's happening? There's smoke coming out of Mount Rainier."

"I think it's going to erupt. Or it has already. I'm not sure. They're not telling me anything here. Are you home? Can you go pick up the boys?"

"Erupt? Are you sure? Hang on, I'm going to turn on the news."

"No. Naomi, this is important. There's no time for that. I'm not sure of anything but I can't leave work right now. Is there any way you can go to the school and get Luke? Pretend to be me if you need to. They shouldn't be there at a time like this, and the roads are going to be chaos."

"Of course. I'm on my way now. There's no way I'm leaving Trevor there."

"Thank you so much, Naomi. You have no idea how grateful I am." Teresa hung up, wishing she could go outside and see what was happening. Even if she went back out to the car though, she'd have to drive down the road to get a view. Jerry barely let her make a call for her kid, there was no way he would let her go outside and take a look around just to satisfy her curiosity.

When Teresa got back to her desk, there was a murmur going around. She noticed an alert on the computer screen.

"URGENT ALERT. Mount Rainier erupted today at approximately 1:04 p.m. Emergency services will be spread thin. Please follow the following talking points."

She let out a breath, then plugged her headset in, thankful to finally have some real information.

CHAPTER ELEVEN

Cascade Middle School

Luke waited impatiently for his turn at show-and-tell. This was the last year he would be able to do it without looking like a baby. Some kids already complained that it was a "little kid" thing, but Luke looked forward to it.

He pretended to be annoyed, along with the other kids, because he didn't want to get teased. If the *cool* kids knew how much Luke liked and looked forward to show-and-tell, he'd never hear the end of it. Things like that followed you to high school and even beyond.

His best friend, Trevor, was in front of the class showing his new Minecraft map.

"Thank you, Trevor. Remember, let's raise our hands, please, guys," the teacher said, after there were several outbursts.

"I'm all done now," Trevor said, heading back to his desk.

Everyone clapped for Trevor's presentation. Luke swallowed the lump in his throat. He was next. He held his painted rock collection close to his chest, ready to head to the front of the room as soon as his teacher called him.

"Let's see who's next on the list." She looked over the class roster then said, "Luke?"

He nodded in her direction and got up, trying to hide his smile. At the front of the room, he felt light headed. Even though he loved show-and-tell, he still felt shy in front of everyone, with all their eyes focused on him.

Luke started to sweat. He worried what they were going to think about his rocks. This morning he'd been so excited, so eager to show everyone. He'd been so *sure* they'd be interested. But now, he was having second thoughts. Maybe the only ones interested were the kids in his rock-painting group.

In the front of the room, holding his clear case to his chest, Luke began. "I-I brought." He gulped when the girls in back started to giggle. "I brought my rocks," he said.

When Luke turned his case over to open the latches, the rocks inside spilled out. The girls in back laughed out loud now, not holding back. "Shh now, girls, that's not nice," the teacher said. She came over to Luke to help him pick up his collection.

Luke tried to hide the tears pooling in his eyes, but she seemed to see right through him. "It's okay," she whispered. "You don't have to present today, if you don't want to."

Full of embarrassment, there was nothing Luke wanted more than to go back to his desk and hide but if he did that, he'd *really* get picked on. He shook his head. "I'll be okay."

As slyly as he could, he wiped his face and took a steadying breath. Luke set the opened case of rocks on the teacher's podium and selected his favorite. It was a Charizard Pokémon, painted in metallic red, with elaborate flames in a circle around it.

He held it in his hand, swallowing the disappointment of being made fun of, trying to forget about being such a spaz. He smiled at the intricate detail of the rock. *Someone put a lot of time into this one,* he thought. He told himself for the millionth time how lucky he was to have found it.

"I love painted rocks—"

"We know!" someone yelled.

"Stop that now. The next one to speak out of turn gets detention," the teacher said, losing her patience. She looked at Luke with sympathy and gave him a nod.

"I collected these with my mom when we went to the park," he said. "This one is Charizard. He's my favorite." Luke held the rock in the palm of his hand and raised it to show the class. When he looked out, he noticed he'd captured some interest.

He continued talking about the rock, explaining why he liked it so much and where he found it. Luke went to put the rock back in its spot in the case and grab the next one. When he did, the rocks in the case started shaking. The whole podium was shaking and when Luke looked, he realized the whole building seemed to be shaking.

The girls in back who had been laughing before, now screamed. "It's okay!" the teacher cried. "Everyone under your desks, now!"

Everyone obeyed without question. Luke rushed from the front to go back to his desk and hide. He held on to the tops of other desks as he walked through the rows, trying to keep his balance.

Under his desk, Luke looked out the window. There was a tree swaying back and forth, along with the telephone lines. When the shaking finally stopped, the teacher reached for the phone.

Minutes later, the teacher addressed the class again. "Guys, we're going to evacuate the school. If you have a cell phone, call your parents now. If you don't have a phone, you can take turns using the class landline."

Everyone started talking among themselves, desperate to

figure out what was happening. The school was *evacuating*. What could possibly happen to make them do that?

"I don't have any information right now, guys. I'm sorry," she said.

"What do you mean? What did they say on the phone?" someone asked.

"Trust me. If I had any information, I would share it."

Luke could see the concern on her face. He trusted her.

Everyone seemed to have a phone but Luke and a handful of others. When it was his turn to use the teacher's phone, he called his mom's cell phone, but she didn't answer. He left her a voice mail, then wondered if he should call 911. He figured she probably wouldn't be the one answering, and he didn't want to get in trouble for calling the number without a real emergency.

"Did you get a hold of your mom?" Trevor asked.

"No. I left her a message. What about you?"

"Yeah, my mom is on her way to come get me. She says she'll pick you up too."

"What about my mom?" Luke asked. He didn't want to go with Trevor only to have his mom worry about where he was.

Trevor shrugged. His mom didn't say anything else about it. "I'm not sure. It's up to you, but I'm sure your mom would want you to get out of here."

Luke decided he would try calling his mom again later. Maybe Trevor's mom had a phone he could borrow.

"Has everyone got ahold of someone to pick them up?" the teacher asked several minutes later. She was in a hurry to get them out of the classroom.

Everyone nodded or called out, "Yes."

"Okay, we're going to wait in the gymnasium for pickup. Please form a line."

THE SILENCE THAT DESCENDED WAS DEAFENING. KIDS WHO normally wouldn't shut up, now had nothing to say. No one said a word as they walked single file through the school halls to the gym.

They piled after each other into the bleachers, next to other classes who did the same. At the bottom of the gym, a group of teachers stood in a circle, whispering to each other, none seeming to pay attention to the kids who were left to themselves in the bleachers.

Luke turned to Trevor. "What do you think happened?" he whispered.

"I'm not sure, but it has to be something big. They wouldn't do this for an earthquake, would they?"

Luke had never felt an earthquake, so he wasn't sure. He didn't want to admit it, not even to his best friend, but he was scared. He wished his mom would've answered the phone. He missed her more than anything.

CHAPTER TWELVE

The classes in the bleachers were organized by grade level. Since Luke and his class were sixth graders, and the youngest, they were at the bottom. Seventh graders were immediately behind them, followed by eighth graders, who thought they were gods, at the very top.

There were four sets of bleachers to hold everyone, two side by side on each end of the gymnasium. Luke looked around, observing the looks on everyone else's faces. Some looked bored, some interested, and a few terrified. He hoped he was hiding the fear in his own eyes. He didn't like how vulnerable those who were afraid seemed.

"Whoa!" screams went out as the bleachers started to shake. There was another quake, this one worse than before.

"Make it stop!" someone at the top yelled.

The kids at the top of the bleachers had it the worst. Some were crying, others holding on for dear life as the old wooden bleachers rocked from side to side. The shaking continued. The lights began to flicker.

Luke heard a loud CRACK and watched in horror as the back of the set of bleachers next to him collapsed. Screams filled the air. Some kids tried jumping over to Luke's set of bleachers on their way down.

Those who jumped, landed on other kids with crushing force, some of them not making the gap and dragging others down with them when they fell. The sudden added weight, in combination with the impact of the other bleachers falling, caused Luke's bleachers to sway even harder.

He heard wood cracking, not loud and sudden like before, but as a slow breaking. "Stop!" Luke cried. "Ours is going to break too!" The tremor hadn't stopped yet, but Luke stood up, ready to climb to the floor. He was only the second row up, but with the panic spreading, he knew he could be crushed just as easily as if he was at the top.

Teachers rushed forward, trying to help kids get down and trying to calm the panic. The quaking finally eased. Hundreds of kids stood and rushed for the staircase at the same time. It was the final straw for the old splintering wood beneath. Like the other set of bleachers, Luke's set collapsed on itself, taking everyone down with it.

Luke's ears were ringing with screams and cries of pain. The kids who were at the top dropped over nine feet to the ground, going down with thousands of pounds of bodies and wood on top of them.

Already at the bottom of the stairs when it went down, Luke was one of the few left untouched. He watched horror-struck as kids piled on top of others, dragging some down, trampling others, all in an effort to get out of the pile of bodies.

Luke was shaking in fear, terrified. The teachers were trying to help but it wasn't enough. *Everyone* was too afraid. No one was thinking rationally. He wanted to help too but was petrified that he'd be dragged to the bottom in the process.

Luke thought about what his mom would do. She would help; he knew it. It wasn't right to stand there and not do anything at all. "Do you have a phone?" He looked at the kid next to him who nodded.

"Call 9-1-1," Luke said. When the kid fumbled for his cell phone, Luke looked toward the other two sets of bleachers across the gym, still standing. Most of the kids on them were trying to get down, some were stock-still, too frightened to move.

"Don't panic," Luke yelled at them. "That's what made the others collapse. Slow down and be careful."

Those who heard Luke over the screaming and cries of their classmates mostly ignored him. But his warning did get through to some. It was better than nothing. He turned back to the collapsed bleachers with piles of bodies trying to get out from under them. Luke swallowed his fear and moved to help. He started by trying to stay on the outskirts of the hysteria, helping a girl stand up who was not pinned down or crushed.

He went to lift a piece of wood off three girls who were pinned. "Help me push up," he instructed.

"I can't!" one cried.

"My arms are stuck," another yelled.

A teacher saw Luke and moved to help him lift. The three girls were able to crawl out, each of them crying from fear and pain.

It didn't take long for adults to start showing up. Those who'd been called to pick their kids up were arriving at the school and being directed toward the gymnasium because of the commotion.

"What happened?" a mother wailed, horrified by the sight. "Did anyone call an ambulance?"

"I did," someone said.

"George!" another woman cried. "George Hernandez! Where are you, son?" She searched through kids' faces, frantic to find her boy. Parent after parent entered the gymnasium and what was already a cluster of panic, grew into mass hysteria.

The fear in the adults' eyes fed the kids' own terror, multiplying until any semblance of order was eliminated. By now, all the kids from the other side of the gym were off their sets of bleachers, mixed in the middle of the building like a mosh pit.

Parents were more worried about finding their own children than helping those who were still crushed and trapped under the fallen sets of bleachers.

Luke continued to try helping as best he could. He wasn't strong enough to keep lifting sections of bleacher by himself, but he tried to keep others from trampling the faces and limbs of those who were trapped. Anyone he could reach, he held their hand, offering even a small amount of comfort.

One boy was completely pinned; the only thing sticking out was the top of his head. Luke touched the boy's hair. Listening to the boy's muffled sobs from beneath, he leaned as close as possible to whisper, "I'm right here."

As Luke kneeled next to the boy, trying not to be dragged under in the hysteria, he scanned for Trevor. Trevor had been sitting next to him toward the front of the bleachers and should've been right behind him on the stairs. Luke didn't see him now, and worried if he'd somehow got trapped with the others.

"Luke!" Luke looked up at the sound of his name. There had to be a hundred other kids with his name at school, but he could've sworn it sounded like a familiar voice.

"Luke!" There it was again. It was Trevor.

"Trev! Over here!" Luke yelled.

"Luke!" Trevor's voice was getting harder to hear. *He doesn't hear me*, Luke thought. He looked down at the top of the trapped boy's head. Guilt clenched his gut as he thought about leaving him to go find Trevor. There was nothing he could do here anyway. If another quake hit, he could be trapped right along with the boy and everyone else who was buried beneath the broken bleachers.

Luke wondered how he would feel if he were in the boy's shoes. If he was alone, trapped beneath a pile of bodies and broken wood, and his only comfort was about to walk away, how would that feel? *Probably pretty scary*, he thought. He couldn't do it. Not until an ambulance showed up at least.

Trevor's voice faded until eventually Luke could hear it no more. He kept his hand on the trapped boy's head as he watched the panic of others. As minutes passed, people filtered out through the doors, slowly emptying the gym.

He kept his hand on the boy's head, providing the only comfort he knew how. Luke couldn't think of anything to say. His throat constricted as he continued listening to the boy's sobbing.

Eventually there were sirens in the distance. "The ambulance is here," he said. "I hear the sirens."

The boy said something unintelligible through his tears.

As the room continued to empty, Luke noticed more adults than kids, which lifted his spirits. "Can I get some help here?" he called out, hoping someone would be able to help him free the boy. He was in pain from being crouched for so long and could only imagine the other boy's pain.

There were still too many others who needed help. Still too many screams filling the air. No one could hear him. Luke assessed the pile again. He could try to move it, but he was afraid of making the wrong move and making things worse. If it collapsed more than it already was, the boy could be crushed into a pulp.

"I'm going to get help," he finally told the boy. Luke stood up to find an adult for help, his knees cracking.

The boy nodded his head a fraction in silent acknowledgment.

"I promise I'll be right back."

CHAPTER THIRTEEN

After leaving their apartment, Jordan and his parents headed toward the Point Defiance Ferry Terminal in Tacoma. Jordan needed to get them as far away from Mount Rainier as he could, without his dad questioning him. Since his mom wanted to ride the ferry, he decided he'd take them to Vashon Island and from there they could keep going north, eventually to Canada.

Almost to the ferry terminal, Jordan's mother said, "Oh, the zoo!" She saw the billboard sign for the zoo and aquarium that was one mile from the ferry.

"Mom, we're about to get on the ferry."

"We haven't bought our ticket yet. Do you think we can go to the zoo first?"

"The zoo? Really? Isn't that for kids?"

She frowned and looked back out the window, saying nothing else about it. Jordan felt a stab of guilt. His mom was a sucker for animals, always had been, even since he was a kid.

"Are you in a hurry for something?" his father asked.

"No, why would I be?" Jordan felt his cheeks redden.

"Your mother wants to go to the zoo. Why not let her? We have nothing else to do."

Jordan clenched his jaw. His father was making him out to be the bad guy, when he was the one trying to save their asses. If shit hit the fan like the news said it would, they would be the ones suffering. Who knew what kind of long-term damage breathing in ash could do? They weren't exactly in perfect health as it was.

He pulled the car past the ferry station to continue around the loop, toward the zoo entrance. *They'll be tired soon enough, then we can continue,* Jordan thought. The zoo had several large hills to climb, and Jordan had a good idea that after one or two of those bad boys, they'd be ready to head back to the car.

"Are you sure you guys can do all that walking?" Jordan asked.

"Of course," his mother answered with a smile. His father looked back out the window, saying nothing, not willing to admit that Jordan was right.

As they descended the first hill, down to the zoo entrance, and the second hill from there, down to the aquarium, the sky darkened, threatening rain. Jordan smiled, thinking it might cut their detour even shorter.

After the hills, seeing the dark clouds overhead, and walking through the aquarium, Jordan's father was reluctant to admit to himself that he was ready to leave. He looked at his wife who seemed to be having a great time and at his son who looked anxious.

"Why do they stink so bad?" Quan asked, holding his nose as they passed the walruses just outside the aquarium.

"It's all the fish they eat," Chun said. She smiled at the grimace on his face.

"I like the one in Seattle better," Jordan said.

"We haven't been there since you were a boy. How can you remember?"

They took their time descending the flight of stairs, down to the outdoor viewing area. A glass wall, eight feet tall, spanned the entire length of the concrete area, displaying the walruses in their habitat.

"They're so majestic," Chun said, smiling.

"They're so lazy," Quan said. "Why are those two just lying there like that?"

Jordan laughed. "They're walruses, Dad. They sleep like cats."

"That one is swimming," Chun added.

The sound of an explosion in the distance startled everyone around. "Was that the military base?" someone asked.

"It was too loud for that," someone else said.

THE GROUND BEGAN TO SHAKE AS THE QUAKE FROM MOUNT Rainier's eruption finally hit. Jordan held on to his parents, hoping they wouldn't lose their balance. The fear in his mother's eyes made him want to punch his father in the face. *How could he put her at risk like this?* Jordan thought.

Seconds into the quaking, he heard a cracking sound that sent dread up his spine. The glass, holding in hundreds of thousands of gallons of water, and three gigantic walruses, was starting to crack.

"We have to get out of here," he whispered to his father.

When Quan looked at him, Jordan nodded to the glass. He didn't want to start a panic. His parents were too old to fight a crowd. He had to get them at least something of a head start up the staircase, before everyone rushed to the exit.

The glass was thick, thick enough to hold back all those millions of pounds of pressure. But was it supposed to crack like that? Jordan didn't trust it and didn't trust his parents' knees not to give out either.

Thankfully, his father understood. "I'm feeling ill," he said. "Let's go, Chun."

She followed without question, holding firmly onto Jordan's arm as he led her up the stairs.

"Dad." Jordan offered his father his other arm.

"Go ahead, I'm right behind," Quan said, holding on to the hand railing.

Jordan and his mother moved forward, taking one step at a time at what felt like a snail's pace. She was trying to hurry, which was making her miss steps. She fumbled, almost falling.

"Easy, Mom, it's okay," Jordan assured her. If she did fall, she was going to take him down with her.

They were halfway up the cement staircase when someone in the crowd below finally noticed the cracking glass. A thin stream of water was leaking through. "The glass is cracked!" someone yelled, setting everyone else in motion.

"Get away from the glass!" another shouted.

There wasn't a lot of people, only about twenty, but when they all headed for the stairs in a panic, at the same time, it could've been a stampede of a hundred.

"Hold on tighter," Jordan told his mom.

The kids were the first to rush past, running up the narrow staircase ahead of their parents. Without holding on to the railing, they swerved around Quan first and then Jordan and Chun.

Jordan glanced back to check on his father, who was still a few steps behind. He saw the sweat beading on his forehead as he looked down at his feet, concentrating on taking one step at a time.

Almost at the top, just a few steps farther, the glass broke completely. Water rushed out in a title wave. "Run!" someone screamed. The crowd started to run up the steps, desperate for their lives.

Jordan pulled his mom forward, trying to get her to go faster the last few steps. As he pulled, others pushed, resulting in a collision. Chun cried out as she fell, hitting her forehead on the top step.

"Chun!" Quan yelled for his wife, but he was being pushed by the crowd too. He was slower moving and by the time he saw what happened to her, the water hit him.

The force was stronger than any blow the crowd could've dealt. Quan was pushed forward into the cement staircase with the spine-crushing force of the water behind him. He was dragged under the surface as he cried out in agony, inhaling saltwater and walrus feces.

Jordan was too busy trying to help his mother to see his father die. He had to get her up before the water hit. He tried picking her up, but she was too heavy, and he wasn't strong enough.

"Mom!" Jordan glanced behind to see the water rushing forward. They had three steps to go then they'd be safe behind the side of the building.

"Jordy, go!" she cried, still trying to stand up.

"Not a chance!"

A man ahead rushed down to help Jordan move his mom. His family was waiting for him, his wife urging them to hurry. They only had seconds before the water hit.

The man was strong enough to move Chun without another thought. Carrying her, he and Jordan rushed the final way up and around the side of the cement building.

The tidal wave crashed down at the top of the stairs, spitting water out of the opening like a tide in a cavern. It was then that Jordan realized his father wasn't there with them. He looked from face to face. "Mom, do you see Dad?"

Chun frowned. "No." She called for her husband. "Quan?"

A woman came forward. "Is that him?" She pointed at a floating body.

The scream his mother let out when she saw her husband's body was like nothing Jordan had ever heard.

Tears sprung to his eyes as he watched his mother, so loving and gentle, so shy and reserved, break down in front of the crowd of onlookers.

This can't be real, Jordan thought. How could his dad be alive one minute and drowned at the zoo the next? He was racked with guilt from the decades-long argument that he and his father shared. From the idea that he was never good enough to take care of them, that he should have tried harder.

This is all my fault, he thought. With the knowledge that his father put him and his mother first every step of the way until the end of his life, Jordan vowed to not let his father down again.

CHAPTER FOURTEEN

I n the middle of the week, in the middle of fall, Jordan couldn't believe how many people were at the damned zoo. He saw tons of kids running for the exit and thought there had to be some kind of field trip going on for there to be so many of them.

"We have to get out of here," he said to his mom. She was still crying into his shoulder, trying to shield her face from looking at Quan's body.

"I can't leave your father," she said through her tears.

"You have to, Mom. Dad would want you to be safe. We're not safe here."

"What about his—" she sobbed. "His—"

"Don't worry about his body," Jordan choked. "What's important is getting out of here *alive*. We can come back for Dad later when this is all over. There could be another quake any time. Or worse."

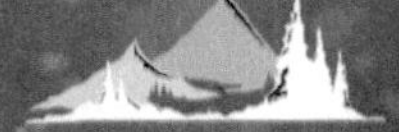

Chun swiped at the tears that wouldn't stop falling. She didn't want to leave her husband, couldn't imagine just leaving him here like this. They had been through so much together in this life. He was her rock. What was she supposed to do without him?

Jordan was right, though. There was already chaos, and it was only going to get worse. She didn't know how she would be able to walk out of there, but she had to. For her son.

"We have to get Chong," she said.

"What? No, there's no time to go back for him."

Chun looked up into Jordan's eyes, determination flashing. "I won't leave him."

Jordan knew he couldn't ask his mom to walk away from her dog. Not now, anyway. Not after what had just happened. He wasn't sure if his mom's heart could take that kind of loss all at once.

He thought of poor little Chong, alone and afraid in their apartment. He was probably curled up into a little ball in his bed, shaking like a leaf. If the quake from Rainier hit this bad in Tacoma, the apartment must've been just as bad, if not worse.

Jordan swallowed the lump in his throat. Anxiety was eating away at him every second they stood there. Wiping his sweaty palms on his pants, he said, "Okay. Let's get out of here."

He helped his mother limp through the crowd of people funneling to the exit. More pushing, more yelling, more panic. He couldn't let her fall again. She'd break a bone if she hadn't done so already. He was worried about the gash in her forehead as it was.

As they slowly came closer to the zoo exit, Jordan watched in terror as people fought each other tooth and nail, trying to get through. People with strollers bashed into the backs of other's legs. Women swung bags at men's faces, men dropped backpacks where they were standing, so they could jump over the entrance gates. The screaming rang in his ears even from this distance.

"We can't go through this way," Jordan said. He couldn't drag his mom through that nightmare.

Jordan spotted an empty wheelchair. It was flipped on its side, outside the gift shop. He only had a moment's hesitation, wondering if someone inside would be missing it before he moved for it. He hoped for the best, but he had to get his mom the hell out of there and he was ready to do whatever needed to be done.

"Sit in this," he said, pulling the wheelchair in front of his mother. He could see the relief written all over her face as she followed his instructions. "Hang on, I'm gonna get us out of here."

Jordan took off at a sprint, away from the crowd, back into the center of the zoo. Chun's hair flew out behind her as Jordan rushed back toward an employee entrance. "Where are we going?" she called back to him. "Isn't the exit that way?"

"I'm going to try getting out through the worker's entrance. Might be less crowded."

He raced down the sidewalk, taking shortcuts across the grass when there were too many people to pass. Jordan was relieved to see that he was right. Everyone was running to the front, leaving no one else in this side of the park.

A few people who weren't in the heart of the crowd took notice of their direction. "Hey, where are they headed?"

Jordan ignored them but slowed his pace as much as he dared. If they realized what he was doing, they would overrun him and his mom and block this exit with their hysteria too. He walked at a fast pace, feeling his spine tingle with the anticipation of footsteps behind.

Nobody followed. Jordan steered his mom through the abandoned employee entrance, spilling out onto a service road. He almost cried from relief. They were out.

"What about the car?" his mom asked.

"Don't worry, we'll walk around. Everyone else is coming from the other direction, so we won't have to fight them." *Hopefully*, he thought.

By some miracle, Jordan was right again. It was farther around, but the mob was on the other side, allowing a wide opening for him and his mom to get through. He thought of his dad, who was left behind, before pushing the thought to the back of his mind. He would let himself feel the regret and pain when this was all over. For now, he had to think of his mom.

Jordan helped her into the car, abandoning the wheel-chair in the parking lot, for anyone else who might find it and need it. He started the car, finally letting relief and hope fill his lungs. "We're gonna get Chong, Mom. Then we're gonna get the hell out of here. One way or another."

CHAPTER FIFTEEN

The zoo exit looped around past the entrance to the ferry terminal that Jordan had wanted to board. As they passed it, in the direction of his parents' apartment, they saw the devastation that was already present.

"Oh my," Chen said, holding a hand to her mouth.

Hundreds of cars were in line to get on the ferry. But they weren't going anywhere because those who'd been there first made some bad choices. They drove their cars onto the boat too fast, and too many.

"They panicked," Jordan said.

Drivers had kept pulling forward until they pushed the cars in front of the ferry off the other side, into the water. They kept coming until they were parked on the ramp, not even on the boat itself. They plowed into the side of the boat, thinking they'd be able to nudge a car or two over to make room.

It was too late. The boat wasn't going anywhere, especially since tidal waves from the quake had it halfway ashore. The cars, with people inside them, were trapped. *How long has it been?* Jordan wondered, amazed that all this had happened in the span of what felt like mere minutes.

"We should've listened to you," Chen whispered.

"There was no way to know."

"We watched that interview on the television. We knew. We just didn't believe."

Even though it was a good feeling to have his mother acknowledge he was right, Jordan couldn't let her blame herself for this. This was a natural disaster. It was mother nature's fault, no one else's. A familiar twinge of guilt filled him, as he thought of how he'd blamed his dad.

"Don't do that to yourself," Jordan said. "Dad was against evacuating, and nothing was going to change his mind." He could still blame him if it would make his mom feel any better. Anything to protect her.

GETTING BACK TO THE FREEWAY WAS NEARLY IMPOSSIBLE. ALL lanes in both directions were stopped for miles. One direction was back toward the ferry that they should've already been on. In the other direction, the freeway.

Jordan weaved the car through neighborhoods and back streets, trying to work his way to the freeway. Stoplights and stop signs were now irrelevant. Jordan and every other driver on the road ignored traffic laws as they tried to get out of the city without crashing.

"Watch out!" his mom cried as another car almost T-boned them on her side of the car.

"Shit!" Jordan yanked the steering wheel and gunned it, almost hitting a different car in the process. Too many people weren't paying attention. And there were too many people, period.

They watched a truck slam into a Prius that then scrunched up like an accordion. Down the road, one woman wasn't paying attention to anything but her phone and drove straight into a house.

Jordan couldn't bear to look at his mom, who was silently crying in her seat, mourning her husband but also afraid for her son's life and her own. Jordan reached to grip her hand. "Don't worry, Mom. It'll be okay."

CHEN DIDN'T ANSWER. SHE SNIFFLED QUIETLY, HOPING HER precious Chong wasn't too scared, feeling the overwhelming guilt of leaving her husband behind. She tried to think of other things, like how much damage there was at home.

She told herself that home was too far from Rainier to have sustained any damage. There would have been a quake shaking things around but that wouldn't cause *that* much damage. Would it? She shook her head, thinking how afraid her poor Chong probably was.

"I'm sorry," she said.

"Mom, I told you already, it's not—"

"I mean, I'm sorry for this. For making us waste time. I'm just so worried about Chong." She started sobbing again, trying, and failing to hide it.

Jordan swallowed the lump in his throat. "Chong is family, Mom. We're not leaving him behind and there's nothing to be sorry for. What I want to know, is how much of your soup was left over from earlier? I'm starving."

Chen couldn't help but laugh. "Not enough, probably."

Jordan smiled. "You're probably right. Think any drive-throughs are open?"

Chen laughed again. Her son had a way of making her feel better. It was a special touch that only he had, and in this moment, she felt so grateful to him. Her eyes shone as she looked at him.

Jordan jerked the steering wheel again, another narrow miss. His forehead furrowed, his shoulders tense, as anxiety coursed through his veins. He was ready to respond in a heartbeat the instant it was needed.

"Something on my face?" he asked, noticing her stare.

Chen shook her head. "No, nothing."

"What is it?"

"I love you, son."

Jordan clenched his jaw, trying desperately not to cry. *I'm a grown man! I do not cry,* he thought. His lips pursed like he'd just eaten a lemon. With eyes pooling, he fought back the emotion, unwilling to let it go.

"I love you too," he ground out.

They rode in silence the rest of the way. Chen lost in her thoughts, Jordan blocking everything out but the road. Neither mentioned Quan.

CHAPTER SIXTEEN

Bleeding, covered in broken glass, Tim reached for Nate. "Are you okay?"

Nate moaned in pain, holding his head. As he did, he noticed the shard of glass sticking out of his hand. Looking at it made him feel faint.

Tim noticed the glass at the same time. "Don't look at it," he said. He held Nate's injured hand in his and slowly, with surgical precision, pulled the glass out.

Nate clenched his jaw, trying not to scream, but the pain won. "Ahhh!" he yelled, tears springing to his eyes.

"Shh now. All done," Tim said. He opened the glove box for some fast-food napkins to hold against the bleeding, brushing past the small revolver that he kept hidden. "I have a first aid kit somewhere around here." He turned around to look in the back seat.

"Can we get out?" Nate asked. He didn't want to throw up inside the truck.

Tim looked around through the windows and rearview mirror. He wanted to make sure it was as safe as possible first. "How's your ankle?"

Nate wiggled his foot. "Fine. Almost forgot all about it."

"Coast is clear. It looks like things are calm enough for

the moment. Let's make it quick if you're sure you're ok. We need to get out of here. Do you need help with your door?"

Nate pulled the handle with his uninjured hand. "Got it."

As they were stepping out, the world seemed to be completely still. The eruption seemed to have dazed everyone. Broken glass littered yards and the road. Some who'd been moving during the blast were now flipped over or crashed.

There were houses on fire, nothing big yet, but the flames were there. Tim grimaced when he saw people dead in their yards. A sinking feeling went straight to his stomach as he thought how much this looked like the landslide he remembered as a kid.

Tim gave Nate some space to empty his stomach, opening the door to the back seat to search for the first aid kit. "Where is that damned thing?" he mumbled to himself, searching through equipment and spare clothes and boots, trying not to get cut by the glass.

He couldn't find it. Tim finally bent down to look under the seat and low and behold, it was there. "Yes!" he yelled, reaching for it.

"Umm, Tim?"

Tim turned at the sound of Nate's worried tone. "Yeah?"

"Should we be worried about the hot lava?"

"No. We're too far out."

"Then what's that?" Tim turned to see what Nate was pointing at. The forest, back toward Rainier, was on fire. Red molten lava was flowing between the trees and down the road, heading straight for them. It was consuming anything in its path, lighting everything that wouldn't melt on fire.

Tim's eyes grew wide as he realized the lava was going much farther than originally predicted. "We've got to get out of here," he said. He looked around at all the other people out of their cars, trying to get their bearings. "Everyone, get to higher ground or get the hell out of here! Lava!" he yelled.

Others began to notice the forest fire and as their gazes traveled down, what was happening registered. People started running in all directions, some heading for houses on the hill next to the road, others taking their chances running farther up the road, in the direction of Elbe, thinking they could outrun the lava. It had to run out of steam eventually.

They scattered like leaves in the wind, only this was more like a tornado. People knocked into each other, swinging fists and clawing. Screaming, yelling, and crying to each other, they showed no mercy to those who were the slowest to move. Tim watched in dismay as some of those with working vehicles were ready to plow down anyone not able to get out of the way fast enough. It was everything he'd been afraid of. It was worse.

"Let's go, kid." They piled back into the Jeep, ready to drive for Elbe. Tim turned the key in the ignition, but the starter wouldn't turn over. "Come on," Tim said, slamming his hand against the dash.

He turned the key again, watching the lava grow closer in the rearview mirror. Again, it didn't start.

"Tim?"

Tim tried a third time, giving the Jeep some gas at the same time. "Come on, goddammit!"

"Tim!" Nate was leaning out the broken window, watching the lava melt cars a hundred yards away.

"One more time," Tim said, turning the key a final time. The ignition started to turn but the engine still wouldn't start. "Fuck!" Tim yelled. "Let's go. Time's up."

He opened the glove box and grabbed the revolver before he and Nate climbed out and ran. With the lava less than fifty yards away, Tim could feel the heat radiating from it. They were both sweating, and it wasn't from the exertion of running.

The molten magma chased after them, melting everything in its path. Down the road, Tim glanced back to check its progress. "Jesus, it's still coming," he huffed, still jogging.

"Isn't that what lava does?"

"It should've stopped by now. We're miles out. At this rate, it's going to run into Elbe and theoretically, they should be way past the lava zone."

They were able to slow their pace now that they were a safe distance from the heat. Tim hoped the people in Elbe would already be evacuated. He could warn them all day, but if they wouldn't listen there was not much else he could do.

Surely they heard the blast, saw the smoke, felt the earth quaking. If they saw all that and still ignored it, there probably wasn't much else he could say to convince them.

Still carrying the first aid kit, Tim looked at Nate. "Let's stop for a second so I can wrap you up properly."

Nate glanced back toward the lava. With fear in his eyes, he said, "I'd rather wait."

"It'll only take a minute. I need to get some ointment on it, so it won't get infected." He looked down at Nate's feet. "Are you sure your ankle is fine? Which one was it?"

Nate looked back again. He didn't want to stop but he did as he was told, offering Tim his injured hand. "I'm fine. I promise."

Tim started to take Nate's hand but stopped as he heard something in the distance. He tilted his head, trying to figure out what he was hearing. He blinked.

"What is it?" Nate asked.

"I'm not sure. I think—"

It was growing louder. No longer a faint noise, now it was like thunder. It was a sound Tim would know anywhere. A memory of his childhood flashed before his eyes.

He was upstairs. In trouble because of his stupid sister. She threw syrup all over everything and Dad got so mad. "This is your fault," he whispered to Melissa through their shared bedroom wall.

He was expecting her to say something back; she always had to have the last word, but there was no response. "Melissa?" he tried again.

Nothing.

Tim sighed, he lay back on his bed. He was so bored. Why did she always have to get him in trouble? He rolled over to look out the window, eyes bulging out of their sockets when he saw the earth rolling toward him, ready to swallow him whole.

"Landslide!" Tim yelled. He grabbed Nate and took off like their lives depended on it.

Tim knew he had to get them off the main road and onto higher ground. The highway they were on followed along the Nisqually River, at least part of the way. The snowmelt, mud, and debris from the top of Rainier were supposed to follow a path down the river, but it was going off the predicted course. Just like the lava wasn't sticking to the plan either.

The river was overflowing. Not only that, but the landslide was coming from other directions too. It meant the evacuation plan was wrong. Dead wrong. Tim didn't have time to think about it, though. With the landslide and lava both coming after them, he wasn't sure if they would make it out of this one alive, let alone make it to warn others.

CHAPTER SEVENTEEN

Waiting on word from Luke was torture. Every minute, Teresa glanced at her phone, expecting to see a message from Naomi, letting her know she had him and everything was fine. With each new call Teresa took on the emergency line, and still no word from her son, her worry grew.

"Ma'am, with the volcano eruption, police and EMTs are stretched thin. I've alerted them to your situation, but it might be a long wait. Is there a safe place you can hide?" she said to the woman on the phone.

"You don't understand! It's not me. It's the kids. They're trapped!"

"Where are they trapped?"

"Under the bleachers! Goddammit aren't you listening? It's Cascade—" The phone cut off.

"Ma'am? Are you there?"

Silence.

Teresa felt the icy hands of fear climbing up her spine. Was the woman talking about Luke's school? She broke out in a cold sweat, rubbing her hands against her legs to dry them off.

Something was wrong and it wasn't just the call being

disconnected. Teresa turned her computer monitor off and then back on again, thinking there was some kind of glitch. The only thing on her screen was a red error message. The entire call system was down.

She took off her headset and turned to the coworker next to her. "Did your system go down too?"

"Yeah. Must be from Rainier."

"But why didn't it go out at first?"

He shrugged. "Someone hit something out there."

Teresa locked her jaw, thinking about Luke. What if the woman on the phone was talking about his school? What if he was one of the ones trapped? What if Naomi was fighting traffic and got into a crash? There was no one to help right now if something happened, and the chances of an accident were exponentially high.

"First responders are stretched too thin," Teresa said.

"Tell me about it. I've been telling people that all day. It's those damned wildfires too. We had to send everyone off to help with those and now look at us."

"I'm sure someone will get this sorted." They both saw through the lie but left it alone. Negativity wouldn't do anyone any good. Teresa looked down at her phone again.

"Hey, hope you guys are okay… what's the update?" She texted Naomi. A second later, the message kicked back. Unable to send. She had no signal. If the whole 911 system was down, and the cell towers too, they couldn't receive calls from anyone, which meant there was no reason for her to be there. They were sitting there waiting on calls that wouldn't come, when she could be out making sure her son was safe. Teresa got up from her desk, on a mission to find her boss.

JERRY WAS IN HIS OFFICE, SITTING AT HIS DESK WITH HIS FEET up and a book in his hands. Teresa knocked at his door even though it was wide open.

"Come on in," he said, setting his book in his lap.

"Jerry, I need to leave," she said, cutting straight to the heart of it.

"No way, Teresa. Sorry, we need you here. I thought we went over this already."

Teresa felt her heart rate increase as her anger toward Jerry grew. She took a breath, trying to control her temper. "But the whole system is down now. What's the point in staying if we can't help anyone? We're just sitting here like lame ducks."

"It could come back up any time," he said. "Then what do we do when everyone's gone home?"

She dug her fingernails into her palms. "Jerry, I'm worried about my son. One of the callers I just had said there was a school with a bunch of kids trapped. I'm worried it's Luke's school. I need to go home."

"Did they say the name of the school?"

She hesitated. "No. The call got cut off—"

"I'm sure everything is fine."

"How can you say that? There's no way to know. Jerry—"

He gave her a condescending smile. "It must be hard being a single mom. Too bad you don't have a man in your life to watch your boy for you."

Teresa bit her tongue. She wanted to slap the look right off Jerry's face. It was the kind of comment he always made, knowing she wouldn't say anything back to him. Knowing she was too afraid of losing her job to defend herself and piss him off.

"I'm leaving," she said. "If you want to fire me, take it up with my union rep." Teresa walked away, not turning back when he called for her, thinking she should've done this much sooner. Even if she was fired for walking out, it would be worth it. She couldn't take another minute of her boss.

The parking garage was still full. Rows of cars filled nearly every space on both levels. Nothing looked out of the ordinary. If she hadn't known the volcano had erupted, Teresa would've thought it was a normal day. Until she pulled to the exit. Then she saw the chaos.

All lanes of traffic, on both sides of the road, were stopped in gridlock. No one moved. She couldn't even pull onto the road because there was no room for her car.

Some people tried driving up on the sidewalks, and every now and then Teresa could see random cars veer off into alleyways, she assumed trying to find a way around traffic. "Which way is the right way?" she asked herself.

Luke's school was in the direction of the freeway, but that was also where the worst part of the gridlock was. She wasn't familiar with any of the back streets in this area but even getting lost had to be better than sitting in this mess. She tried to think. If Naomi was able to get the boys, where would she go? Would she take them back home?

Teresa finally decided she would head to Luke's school and go from there. If there was an accident there, it's possible that's where he still was. And if not, the school might have more information for her and maybe even a note left from Naomi.

"I can't believe I'm going to do this," she said as she pulled her car onto the sidewalk of downtown Tacoma.

There was honking as she passed stopped cars, but she wasn't sure if it was directed at her or other cars that wouldn't move. Some pulled onto the sidewalk behind her, and some saw her in their rearview mirror and moved to block her from going around. "Come on!" she cried as a truck intentionally pulled halfway onto the sidewalk and stopped.

It wouldn't fit the whole way on, like her small car did, so it stayed halfway on, blocking her from passing. She honked her horn and threw up her hands. The driver of the truck reached an arm out the window to give her the bird.

Tears threatened to spill as hopelessness overwhelmed her. She'd been so stupid to think she could get around traffic. Teresa was so worried about Luke; she couldn't bear the thought of something happening to him and not being able to get to him. She admonished herself for not trying to get to him sooner. If she would've left when she first thought of it, she wouldn't have had to deal with the traffic like this.

Teresa sat still, watching the other drivers out the window. Some were getting out to abandon their vehicles and walk. She was about to do the same when she glanced in her mirror and saw a delivery truck barreling on the sidewalk behind her and several other cars.

"Oh God," she whispered, watching it smash into everything in its path. Garbage cans, newspaper holders, parking meters, all went flying in the truck's wake. It was about to plow into the car at the back of her line, but instead, it drove straight into the building.

Without losing momentum, the truck barreled through the front of a jewelry store, continuing through each neighboring store like it was made of papier-mâché. When there was a spot on the sidewalk, it blasted out of the store it was in, cutting across to the sidewalk and continuing on its way.

She didn't have to think about it. Teresa turned her wheel to follow behind. "Lead me to the freeway, buddy," she said, finally able to smile.

The driver of the truck seemed to read her mind. He led her straight to the on-ramp of interstate five. When the on-ramp was in sight, she clenched the steering wheel harder. Cars were lined up for miles, dead stopped on the freeway. No one was moving. It was worse than downtown.

"No!" Teresa cried.

She needed I-5 north, only for a minute, then she'd practically be home free. She couldn't go this way now. Not with traffic stopped like this.

The truck she was following seemed to need the southbound on-ramp. He was gone, with no one else to lead her. Other cars at the intersection seemed to notice the same thing she did. A few took the on-ramp, ignoring the traffic. Others turned around.

Teresa rolled down her window to talk to some of the other drivers turning around. "Which way do we go?"

"Try Pacific Avenue. River Road is backed up too," a man said. "Try to follow me, if you want."

"Thanks so much!" she called back. Teresa didn't know how he was going to get through this mess but maybe he knew something about maneuvering his vehicle that she didn't. She was happy to follow anyone who seemed to know what they were doing in a situation like this, and this man was one of those people. It was worth a shot, anyway.

Teresa said a silent prayer for Luke. "Mommy's coming, baby."

CHAPTER EIGHTEEN

Sitting on the front lawn of the school, Luke looked at the boy next to him. For someone who was just trapped beneath broken bleachers, he seemed to look pretty normal. "So, what's your name?" the boy asked. He looked down, shy now and embarrassed to have been seen crying, especially by a little sixth grader.

"Luke. What's yours?"

"James." James looked at Luke now, meeting his eyes. "Thanks for—you know." He waved his arm toward the gym. "You didn't have to stay with me like that. You could've left."

Luke shrugged. "I wouldn't want to be left. So, I stayed."

"Yeah. Well, thanks." James blushed. His eyes shifted away again.

"I'm glad you're not hurt too bad," Luke said. "I wonder when the ambulances will come back."

"Are you kidding? They're not coming back."

"Why not?"

"The frickin' volcano erupted." James shook his head. "We're lucky they showed up at all. They got who they could and bounced, man. They've got bigger fish to fry than us."

"But there're some kids who are really hurt."

"Yeah. And what about the ones cooked by the lava?"

Luke was silent at that. He hadn't thought about all the other people who might be in trouble, but it made sense. There were only so many people who could help, and probably a lot more who were hurt. "Are you able to walk?" he asked.

James moved his leg and wiggled his toes. Although he'd been piled under the bleachers, he was almost unharmed, only suffering minor cuts and bruises as far as he could tell.

"Yeah, I think so," James said. "Where are we headed?"

"I want to find my mom. She works in Tacoma. I'm not sure if she's headed here to pick me up or not, but I'm hoping I might find her along the way. Are your parents coming for you?"

James shook his head. "Nope. They're on vacation."

"Without you?"

"It's their anniversary." He shrugged, trying to act like he didn't mind, but Luke could clearly see that he did. "Anyway, let's go. After what you did for me, I owe you."

LUKE DIDN'T WANT JAMES TO OWE HIM ANYTHING, BUT HE WAS glad for the company. He was also glad James was older and bigger. It made him feel a little safer. He could almost laugh thinking about how he hadn't even wanted to walk along the sidewalk alone that morning and was now about to walk with a boy he didn't know, all the way into Tacoma.

"Do you know how to get there?" Luke asked.

"Sort of. We can't walk along the freeway, that would be too dangerous. So, we're going to try to find River Road."

"Okay. Do you know where *that* is?"

James frowned. "Not really. But I know which way to walk."

"That's good enough for me."

They walked north, toward the direction they believed to be River Road. James knew it would take them all the way to downtown if they could find it. And the good news was, there were sidewalks at various points along it. It was a far safer road to travel along than the freeway.

After a few blocks, as they came closer to downtown Puyallup, the boys noticed the traffic congestion. Cars were swerving in front of other cars, some cutting onto the sidewalk as they tried to go around others.

"Watch out!" James cried, yanking Luke back just in time. The driver in the car in front of them decided to drive across the sidewalk while turning the corner.

"Thanks," Luke panted. He'd been checking the crosswalk signal, not expecting a car to drive up onto the curb. "People are nuts today!"

"People are nuts every day." James smiled.

They both laughed then, scared, relieved, and hopeful. Luke thought about how glad he was to have found James. He hoped he would still be his friend when this was all over.

"Hey, look!" Luke cried, pointing his finger ahead.

James turned his head to see the line of cars stopped ahead. It was worse than anything they'd seen so far. People were getting out of their vehicles and walking in the opposite direction, some running.

The boys stopped walking. "What should we do?" Luke asked.

"I'm not sure." They waited there, watching the events play out in front of them. People left their car doors opened as they carried their belongings. Mothers carried children while babies cried. One man was helping an old woman in a wheelchair. He was too far to know for sure, but Luke thought he saw fear on everyone's faces.

"I wonder if that's the road we need," James said.

"I'm scared, James."

James looked at Luke. "I am too. But what else can we do? You still want to find your mom, right?"

Luke thought about it. Maybe his mom was stuck on the other side. Or maybe she was trying to get to him. He wasn't sure what to think. He thought he had to at least try to get to her. What if there was an accident, like at school, and she was trapped at work?

Thoughts raced through his mind of all the things that might've happened to her. Reasons why she wouldn't have been at the school to pick him up, as he failed to remember that he hadn't reached her on the phone.

Images of his mom's building collapsing flooded his mind. The parking garage crumbling on top of her car, a crazy gunman shooting everyone in her building. What if she was crushed and needed someone to pull her out or hold her hand, just like James?

"Let's go," Luke said.

They walked between cars, heading straight down the road in the opposite direction that people were running. "Excuse me, what's going on?" James tried to call out to several people; none stopped to explain.

Now they were close enough to hear the roaring water of the Puyallup River. "It's the river," James said. "We must be close to River Road." As he said this, he looked confused.

"What's wrong?"

"I'm just a little turned around, that's all." He looked around then back behind them. "I thought we were supposed to walk under the freeway before we got to the river."

Luke shrugged. "I'm not sure, but I hear it. We're close, that's for sure."

They continued walking around a curve in the road when they heard shouting. "Run!" A man was screaming at them, waving his hands above his head as he headed straight toward them. The boys looked at each other, both with panic in their eyes. Luke could feel his heart in his throat. He gulped.

"What's wrong?" James asked the man as he came closer.

"Get the hell out of here!" the man cried. "It's coming!"

Luke and James looked in the distance to see what he was going on about. They saw it instantly. It was what they'd been hearing. It was the river, like they'd thought, but it wasn't *just* the river.

The Puyallup River had overflowed from the landslide off Mount Rainier. Millions of gallons of water, mud, rocks, trees, and other debris were rushing toward them. It had already wiped out part of the city, and it wasn't going to stop anytime soon.

Luke was dumbstruck by what he saw, almost losing control of his bladder. "Come on, we gotta go!" James yelled, pulling at his arm. They turned to run back the way they'd come, as fast as they could. The man who'd been yelling at them to run was now growing farther away, since they were able to run much faster than he could.

"Where do we go now?" Luke asked, still running.

"As far away from *that* as possible," James huffed. He wasn't as good a runner as Luke and struggled to keep up.

"Help! Oh, God, help me!" The boys slowed to see the man behind them about to get swallowed up by the landslide. There was nothing they could do but try to run faster.

"I can help him," Luke said, starting to head back toward the man.

"No way, Luke! You'll never get to him in time."

"We can't just—"

The man fell silent as he was swept away with the

current, held under by fallen trees. Within seconds, he was out of sight. The river was still coming closer, almost upon them.

"There!" James cried. A group of people were climbing up a fire escape on the side of a two-story building. "We need to get to higher ground."

James led Luke to the fire escape in back, where they climbed to the top. As they reached the roof, hands of strangers helped pull them up. Seconds later, the group watched the river flow past, encompassing everything around.

Luke and some of the others cried as ash started raining down.

CHAPTER NINETEEN

Climbing through yards and empty houses was the only way Tim and Nate could move forward. They were lucky enough to be safe on a hill but had to keep moving. The landslide from Rainier had swallowed everything in its path, including the road. There was a new river now and it was at the base of the hill they were currently on.

"Over here," Tim said. "There's a gap between these boards." The gap was small but was just enough for him to get a grip on a wooden plank and pull. Nate winced at the loud break of the wood.

"Can you fit?" Tim asked.

"Yeah. Can you?"

"I think so."

Tim just squeezed through when they heard barking. "A dog!" Nate cried.

"He'll be fine."

"But what if he's not? Can we at least check it out?"

Tim didn't think they had time but couldn't resist the look on Nate's face. The kid had been through a lot today, not just living through a natural disaster, but getting left behind with his classmates too. He couldn't help but want to do something to make his day a little less grim. "Fine. But let's make it quick," he said.

Nate led the way through the empty house, to the front yard. The barking grew louder the closer they came to the flowing slide. "There!" Nate shouted, pointing at a man who was pulling a yellow Labrador by a chain.

It looked like he was trying to get the dog *into* the river. The man would yank, pulling the dog forward so hard it lurched and nearly fell. The dog fought back with every pull, slowing the man down some but it wasn't enough to stop him altogether.

"Hey!" Tim yelled.

The man turned to face them. "What?" he puffed, out of breath.

"What are you doing with that dog?"

"Mind your own damn business," the man said. He yanked the chain, pulling the dog forward again. The dog gave a yelp of surprise in response, again almost falling.

"Is that your dog?" Tim asked. "It looks like he's in pain when you yank on him like that."

"Why don't you fuck off and mind your own business?" The man turned his back toward Tim and Nate, continuing on his path toward the overflowing river. The water, mud, and debris were moving so fast, they seemed to suck down anything in the way. Tim knew if the man got the dog down there, it wouldn't stand a chance trying to pull itself out.

Tim opened the first aid kit and pulled out the revolver. Aiming it into the air, he cocked the trigger. "Cover your ears, kid." Nate obeyed, then Tim squeezed.

The blast from the gun sent the man flying to the ground in fear. He threw his hands up to cover his head, letting go of the dog's chain in the process. The dog didn't waste a moment. He sprinted toward Tim and Nate, cowering behind their legs when finally reaching them.

Nate leaned down to give comfort. He stroked the dog from head to tail, rubbing his fingers through the golden fur. "Hey boy, it's okay now. We won't let anything bad happen to you."

It didn't take the man long to realize he wasn't shot. Looking down, he patted himself and found he wasn't injured or bleeding. With murder in his eyes, he turned toward Tim. "What the fuck did you do that for?"

Tim leveled the revolver at the man, daring him to try anything. "Is there a problem?" he asked.

"That fucking dog is a nuisance. I'm getting rid of him and you're not going to stop me."

Tim's eyes went wide in disbelief. "So, you're what? Going to drag him to his death? Because he *annoys* you?"

"It's none of your business. You can stay the hell out of it and go on your way. You're lucky I don't call the cops for you shooting at me."

"What the hell is wrong with you?" Tim grimaced in disgust. "You need help."

The man's eyes shone with the want of revenge and hate. "Fuck you! I need help? I'll show you how much help I need." He stood, looking ready to charge at Tim.

Tim cocked the trigger. "You are a terrible human being. You don't deserve to lick the dirt off that dog's paws. Let's go, Nate. Bring the dog."

Nate took the chain from around the dog's neck so he could breathe better. The dog gave him a lick of thanks and happily followed when they began to walk away.

"Hey!" the man shouted. "You can't just leave!" He took a step toward them.

"Don't make me use this," Tim said.

The man stopped in his tracks, glowering.

"Don't worry, I'll be sure to let his owner know what you were prepared to do, when this is all over." Tim smiled. "Go ahead and call those cops. I'm sure they'd love to hear all about this little incident."

They left without looking back.

THEY WERE FORCED TO STAY ON HIGH GROUND FOR MILES, AND because of the rural area there weren't houses the whole way. It meant Tim and Nate were hiking for hours through a combination of residential yards and forest, until the path of the landslide veered off and they finally reached a road that wasn't covered in debris.

As they hiked, they both coughed from the buildup of ash and smoke in the air. "Cover your face with your shirt," Tim instructed. It helped a little but was still hard for Nate to breathe.

"We need to find a car, and fast," Tim said. It would allow them to get some filtered air and get them into Seattle, which is where he needed to be.

"How are we gonna get a car?"

"I'm sure someone left the keys in one. Keep your eye out."

When the dog yipped in agreement, Nate laughed and then coughed again. "Okay boy, you keep your eye out too."

Tim stopped at the end of a driveway. "Let me see your hand."

Nate handed over his injured hand that was still bleeding from the glass cuts.

"No more putting this off." Tim bandaged the hand with his first aid kid, to the best of his ability. "I'm going to try walking up this driveway," he said. He pointed across the street. "Do you think you can walk up that one and see if there are any cars unlocked in the driveway?"

Nate nodded, eager to help. "Yeah, I can do that."

"Don't try to start it if there is one. Just come get me."

Nate headed toward the indicated driveway, head lowered, nose tucked under his shirt. Tim did the same to the opposite driveway, hoping they'd come across something soon. The ash and smoke were only going to get worse. Eventually their lungs would get clogged. They needed to get the hell away from this volcano.

TIM HURRIED UP THE DRIVEWAY, HATING TO LEAVE THE KID alone, but hoping one of them would find a usable vehicle faster if they split up. He kicked the gravel up as he walked, following the winding driveway through the forest. He coughed, trying to breathe in as little ash as possible.

Tim wasn't sure how long the driveway was because he couldn't see the house, but he hoped it wasn't too much farther. Huddled into himself against the ash and the chill, he looked around, noticing the lack of wildlife. He stopped. There was a growling coming from inside the trees. Sweat pricked Tim's forehead as he felt whatever animal was in there, watching him.

It was like nothing he'd heard, from an animal he couldn't identify—almost malevolent. "Hey there," Tim whispered in as soothing a voice as he could manage. He felt fear like he'd never known, not even as a child in a landslide. He didn't know if he should run or if that would set the creature off. What if it was a cougar or mountain lion? Hell, it didn't matter what it was, it obviously wanted him for lunch, and he didn't want to tempt it.

Tim put his hands up over his head, trying to make himself appear bigger. He had to cough again but tried to hold it back. "Hey there," he said, this time a little louder. He took a slow step forward. The growling stopped. Tim took another step. He released a breath then took a third slow step.

Movement came from the trees, almost causing Tim to lose his bladder. He was a brave guy most of the time, but when it came to potentially getting eaten alive by a wild animal, he was as good as a baby. "Hey, there!" he called a third time, on the verge of taking his chances running the rest of the way up the driveway.

Then a gray cat stepped out. It looked up at Tim with large, glowing yellow eyes and said, "Meow."

Tim laughed. "Was that you who scared me half to death?" He couldn't believe it was a little house cat that had sounded so loud, so... evil. He leaned down to pet the cat. Tim scratched behind his ears then looked at the tag on his collar. "Hi Shadow, nice to meet you, buddy."

Shadow purred while rubbing against Tim's legs. He walked in a circle around him, then headed back into the forest. "Hey," Tim called. "Come back here, it's not safe!" He started to run after the cat, who he could no longer see. But he heard that growl again. Tim's spine prickled. It was not as bad as before; this time seemed to be more of a warning, but Tim wasn't about to *not* listen. *How can that cat be making this sound?* he wondered. "Okay, okay, hope you know what you're doing, cat."

Without another beat, Tim continued up the driveway. Another bend led him to the garage and house. "Thank you," Tim said, exhaling the breath he'd been holding. He took several deep breaths of clean air inside the garage. The driveway was empty of vehicles, but Tim smiled when he saw what was parked inside.

A black 1969 Dodge Challenger with a 426 Hemi sat in pristine condition. "Well, hello," Tim said, unable to keep from grinning at his luck. He walked to the driver's door, hoping the beauty started.

He checked the glove box for a key, then the center console. No luck. He looked all over the cab, then flipped down the visor. A set of keys fell into his lap. "Woo-hoo!" Tim cried, clapping his hands. "We're in business, baby!"

He stuck the key in the ignition and turned. It started to turn over but hesitated. Tim tapped the gas pedal and turned the key again. A little more gas, then the engine roared to life. He tapped the gas again for good measure. The engine revved, smoke blowing out the tailpipes.

Minutes later, Tim was picking up Nate and the dog. "It's too loud for him," Nate said between coughs.

"Just get in, kid. Not a time to be picky."

Nate frowned but climbed inside with the dog.

"Now, let's get the hell out of here. Hang on." When Tim floored the gas pedal, the back end of the Challenger fish-tailed, swiveling from side to side as the tires tried to grip the pavement. The engine roared, and he shifted through the gears, heading toward Seattle as fast as the car would take them.

CHAPTER TWENTY

Jordan covered his and his mom's faces as he led her to the front door of her apartment. Ash was falling like snow now, covering everything, and making it hard to breathe.

Chen struggled with the front door. "It won't open."

"Is it the lock?" Jordan stepped over to help her. He turned the key, but it was the whole door that was jammed in the frame. He leaned against it, pushing with his full body weight but it still wouldn't budge. "It must be from the quaking."

Jordan took a couple of steps back before rushing at the door and banging into it with his shoulder.

"Don't do that!" Chen cried.

There was a loud pop when his shoulder met the door. It wasn't from the wood. Feeling like an idiot, Jordan stepped away again, holding his injured arm.

"Are you hurt?" She reached for him.

"I'm fine, Mom." The only thing that really hurt was his pride.

Inside the apartment, Chong was barking.

"We're coming, boy!" Chen called. "How will we get in?"

Jordan thought for a minute. "We could go through the back door."

Chen frowned. It would mean breaking the glass but what other choice did they have? She hesitated but finally nodded. "Okay."

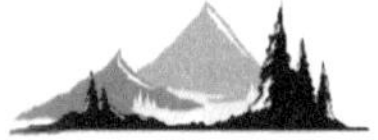

JORDAN BROKE THE SLIDING GLASS DOOR WITH A LARGE ROCK, then using his mother's gardening tools on her patio, cleared enough glass to climb through. "Wait here, Mom. I'll grab Chong."

"But my things—" She choked back a sob. "Your father's things."

Jordan couldn't bear to look at her. He turned away, looking inside the apartment. Boxes that were stacked earlier were now fallen, cupboard doors were open, the apartment looked a mess from where he stood. He didn't see Chong but could still hear him yipping at the front door.

"I'll help you through," he said.

BACK IN THE CAR, JORDAN WAS FIGHTING THROUGH TRAFFIC again, worse now than it had been earlier. Most people on the main roads were at a dead stop, except for those swerving around everyone else, taking sidewalks and side streets to find a way around the congestion. Jordan was one of those people.

"Where are we going?" Chen asked.

"Everyone is heading south, to Oregon, so we're going to try north to Canada, as far as it takes to outrun the ash and smoke."

"What about east?"

Jordan shook his head. "No, I think the majority of the smoke is probably headed that way."

Jordan knew better than to try getting on any kind of freeway or highway. It would be impossible to get anywhere. He stuck to the back streets for as long as he could, trying to maneuver the car east first, and then would go north once they reached Puyallup.

As Puyallup grew nearer, he flicked the windshield wipers to go faster but they were already maxed out and the ash was still piling up. They started to pass more and more people headed in the opposite direction. Ten cars grew to twenty, that grew to a line stretching into the horizon.

"What's going on now? Mom, turn on the radio. Try to find a news station."

Chen reached for the dial. An emergency broadcast was playing on every station. "This is an emergency alert. This is not a test. Repeat, this is not a test. Mount Rainier has erupted, causing significant damage to local areas. Landslides are currently blocking many of the roadways in Pierce County. Ashfall can be hazardous, especially to those with breathing conditions. Please evacuate the area safely. If you are in the cities of…"

"Landslides?" Jordan said, turning the radio back down. He glanced at his mom.

She shrugged. "There was a lot of snow on the mountain. It had to go somewhere."

"Yeah, but that's what the rivers are for—hang on!" He reached across to hold his mom back as he slammed on the brakes. A car passed, the driver laying on the horn with one hand and flipping them off with the other. "Are you okay?" he asked.

Chen nodded. "I'm fine. The Puyallup River is up the road, isn't it? The direction these cars are leaving?"

Jordan thought about it. "I guess so. But it doesn't mean anything."

"I guess we'll find out, won't we?"

It wasn't long before they did find out. When they reached Puyallup, both their jaws dropped when they saw the flooded city. "Oh my," Chen said, holding a hand over her mouth.

Jordan stopped the car, unable to drive any farther. The streets were covered with water so deep he didn't know if the car would even drive through it. It looked like the river was flowing right through the city. In the distance, there were people on a rooftop, waving their arms in the air, calling for help.

"Can we help them?" Chen asked.

Jordan glanced at the tiny back seat. He looked back at the people helplessly stuck on the rooftop. He wanted to say no. They needed to continue trying to get out of the state. If they stopped for everyone who needed help, they'd never get out. But when he looked at his mother, he wanted to make her proud. He wanted to be someone she could be proud of, and a selfish coward didn't fit the bill.

"How would we even get to them?" he asked. "I think the water is too deep to drive through."

Chen pursed her lips. "Stand on top of the car and yell at them. Maybe they have an idea."

"They're at least a hundred yards away, maybe more."

"So, yell loud."

Jordan opened his door, stepping into the ankle-deep water. He gulped, looking into the distance. It only got deeper, and there was a current ahead, flowing *through* buildings. Trees and debris flowed through the city like it didn't even exist.

Jordan took a deep breath then realized how dumb that was with all the ash falling. He coughed at the burning of his lungs. He covered his nose with his shirt, trying to calm his racing heart. When he could finally breathe again, Jordan climbed on top of the car.

"Hey!" he yelled. He waved his arms in the air to match the other people.

"Help us!" He heard their faint reply. From this distance, it was hard to count the number of people, especially with the ash blocking his vision, but it looked like a relatively small group. Maybe ten. Even with that many, he didn't think he'd be able to help them all.

Some would fit in the back, even if they had to squish in, but what about the others? It's not like they could all fit on the roof. That wouldn't work either. "How can I get you?" he called.

The people on the roof talked among themselves. Then someone called, "Sporting goods store. There!" They were pointing into one of the shopping centers nearby.

"What about it?" Jordan yelled back without thinking. He was not a sportsman and not familiar with what was inside a sporting goods store, or why they would point him to one.

"They have boats!"

Ooh, he thought. Now it made sense. He could row over to the people and at least get them out of the water if nothing else. It would save them. He couldn't imagine how long they'd already been in that situation. He wondered if they were starving or thirsty. They had to be, and probably freezing too.

The store was closer to them, meaning deeper water. The problem was, Jordan didn't know *how* deep it was. The water didn't seem to be flowing as much there, which was a good sign. But he didn't know if he could put his mom at risk to save a bunch of strangers.

"I'll try!" he yelled to them. Cheers went up, making Jordan feel like a hero, even though he hadn't done anything yet. He climbed back down off the roof of the car to tell his mom the plan.

"Let's do it," she said.

"But what if the water is too deep? I can't put you at risk."

Chen held her son's hand and looked into his eyes. "At least we'll try. Think of what would happen if no one helped anyone else because of the inconvenience. We don't want to live in that kind of world."

It was all the motivation Jordan needed. Without another word, he started the car and headed toward the sporting goods store.

CHAPTER TWENTY-ONE

As he pulled into the shopping center, Jordan wished he was driving a truck instead of a compact car. He could feel the water in the wheel wells pulling at the tiny car, forcing his steering wheel in the opposite direction. He tried to go slow, but when he heard the tailpipe spluttering in back, he parked the car.

"This is as far as we get."

Chen looked around. "This is good. We're not that far."

She was right. They were in the back of the parking lot now, close enough to walk. Jordan started to sweat with nerves. He wanted to tell her he'd changed his mind. This was a stupid, crazy idea and it was never going to work. He wanted to turn the car around and keep going.

He needed to get her to safety. Not just for her, but for his dad too. But even more than those things, he wanted his mom's eyes to shine when she looked at him. He couldn't have that with his dad now, but it wasn't too late for her. All these years he'd been living for himself. Well, here was his chance to step up.

Jordan wiped the sweat from his brow, refusing to let his mom see how much he didn't want to be doing this. He nodded then opened his door.

"Jordy?"

He turned back. "Yeah?"

"I love you, son. I'm so proud of you."

Jordan smiled. It was the second time she'd said it in such a short time span. Something he couldn't remember happening his entire life. "I love you too, Mom."

He stepped into the water that was now shin high. There was a current, more than he'd expected, but he vowed to walk until it became a struggle. One foot in front of the other, Jordan headed for the storefront into deeper water with each step. He coughed into his shirt again. *I hope they have masks,* he thought.

A hundred feet from the front door, Jordan was swept off his feet when debris flowed into him. He'd been focused on what was displayed in the front window, without realizing the current was picking up.

When he lost his footing, he went under without taking a breath. He kicked and reached, trying to get back up but was turned around in the dark water. He'd lost his bearings on up and down and could feel himself floating away.

"Jordy!" He could hear his mother's faint cries even under the water.

Eventually, he smacked into something hard that stopped his movement. Jordan reached out to hold on to whatever it was, hoping it would hold his weight. Oxygen deprived; Jordan's brain wasn't going to be able to hold out much longer without air.

Holding on with all his might, he was able to pull himself to the surface and take a breath of ash-filled air. He coughed and spluttered, then looked around for the car with his mom still in it.

"I'm okay!" he called to her, waving. The water had delivered him right to the storefront. Jordan was holding on to one of the sliding open front doors. Now that he could stand up again and was able to get his bearings, he found he could still walk through the store as long as he held on to things for stability.

Half swimming, half walking, Jordan headed for the back of the store, where kayaks were hanging on the wall. "They better have something bigger than that," he said, wishing he knew exactly how many people were up on that rooftop. He wondered what they would do if he was only able to take a couple of them at a time.

"I guess I can always make multiple trips," he thought out loud. He scrunched up his face at the thought, not really wanting or having that much time to spend on this rescue mission.

When he finally reached the kayaks, he scoured the nearby area, searching for anything else that might work. There was a blow-up raft that would hold six adults and came with its own oars, a tow-behind inner tube that would hold several, and hanging from the ceiling, was a giant inflated river float that would hold at least ten adults and possibly more. "Holy shit," Jordan said, looking at it and wondering how he could get it down.

Even if he could get the thing down, how would he get it out of the store? It was *perfect* but also impossible. Jordan clenched his fists at his situation. He bit his lips as he tried to decide which would be the best option.

He thought the kayaks would be best because of the hard plastic. They would be more stable, and he wouldn't have to worry about popping it and sinking. But they only held two people, even three or four if they were hanging off the sides but that was max.

Jordan made his way to the stand that held boxes of inflatable rafts. Portable air pumps and batteries were right next to it. His final decision made, he grabbed a raft, a pump, and the necessary batteries, then went back to the kayaks. "Okay, Jordan, buddy, don't screw this up."

He reached for the biggest kayak he could carry and pulled it down from the display. It was heavy, bulky, and wobbled in his arms. Jordan struggled holding it over his head but was able to bring it down without crashing. He took the air pump with batteries now inside it, and the boxed-up raft, and set them inside the kayak along with a set of oars.

On his way out the front of the store, Jordan stopped by the vending machine. "Why not?" he said, breaking into it and putting as much of the food inside the kayak as would fit in the side compartment.

He took a deep breath of fresh air before finally walking out the door. He climbed inside the kayak and started to paddle. As he came closer to his mom, he waved to her, and she gave a reassuring wave back. Jordan smiled to himself, blushing a little when his mom blew him a kiss. He wasn't a kid anymore, hadn't been for a long time now, but it still felt good to be babied by his mother sometimes.

"Hey man, there's twelve of us up here!" Jordan heard some of the people on the rooftop calling as he rowed closer.

"What the hell is that thing supposed to do?"

"Go back and get a bigger boat!"

Jordan ground his teeth, trying to keep from yelling at the ungrateful idiots who would criticize him when he was trying to save their asses. He focused on rowing against the current. He'd never been in a kayak before, and never in a river either, so he was trying to give all his attention to not rowing in circles.

"Almost here," someone called several minutes later. They sounded right on top of him. Jordan looked up from the water and saw that he was only a few feet away now. Almost close enough to touch the building. He bent his neck back to see several peering over the edge of the rooftop.

"I have another boat," he said. "I just have to blow it up."

"Thank God," several said.

Clapping and cheering went around. Several more said, "Thanks, man!"

Jordan opened the raft and started to inflate it. Minutes later, it was a full-size raft in the water, next to his kayak. "Go around back to the fire escape," someone said.

Jordan wrapped a short rope around his waist, pulling the raft behind as he rowed toward the back of the building. He helped people down as best he could, trying to keep both boats from flipping. "Hold my hand," he instructed a woman climbing down.

She took his hand gratefully before stepping into the raft and taking hold of one of the oars. Several more climbed down until the inflated raft was full. "How many more are up there?" Jordan asked the last man who climbed down.

"Just two kids. Thanks again, man." He took the other oar in hand, and they began to row away.

"That's that, then," Jordan said to himself, watching them go. He wasn't sure what he was expecting but didn't understand why they would leave without making sure the kids up there were safe.

Jordan waited, expecting the kids to come down but when no one did, he called, "Hey up there, come on, let's go."

No response came. Jordan looked around, but in the back of the building there was nothing to see but other buildings. He thought about climbing up to see what was going on. "What a pain," he complained.

He took the small rope that had been tied to the inflated raft and tied it from the bottom step of the fire escape to his kayak so it wouldn't float away. Then, Jordan headed up the stairs.

CHAPTER
TWENTY-TWO

As soon as he was high enough up the ladder to see the rooftop, Jordan gasped, then choked on the ash he gulped down. The two kids that the man had mentioned were tied up, bound together with what looked like *jackets*. Their mouths were gagged with socks. "What the hell?" Jordan rushed the rest of the way up.

Both boys were trying to yell through their gags, but Jordan couldn't make out what they were trying to say. "Hang on, hang on." He pulled out bunched-up socks from one boy then moved to untie him.

The boy coughed, inhaled, then coughed some more. Finally, he spit out, "Your car!"

Dread shot through Jordan like a thunderbolt. "What?" He stood up and ran to the edge of the rooftop, trying to find his car in the distance. It took him a second, but he finally saw it. The others in the raft were rowing straight for it. "Fuck!"

The first boy was finished untying the second boy. "We tried to stop them," the second boy said.

Jordan understood the situation and was angrier now than ever. His mom was still in the car and if those people touched her, he wouldn't let them get away with it. "We gotta go, guys," he said.

They started back for the ladder, carefully climbing back down to the waiting kayak. "It'll be a tight squeeze," Jordan said, picking up the oars. One boy sat next to Jordan, and the other was sitting halfway on top of him, with his legs hanging out of the boat.

"Do either of you know how to row?" Jordan asked.

Both boys shook their heads. "Alright then, guess that leaves me." It was clumsy going with the weight and not being able to see, mixed with smoke and ash still coming down, and not being able to breathe. Jordan did his best to row as fast as possible, realizing that the others would get to his mom first. He just hoped they left her in peace. There was nothing he could do about the car, but he hoped they would leave the old woman alone.

"My name is Luke, and this is James," the kid sitting next to Jordan said, pointing to his friend who was halfway off the kayak.

Jordan wiped sweat from his brow. "Jordan."

They were out from behind the buildings now, with a clear view of the car. The others had already parked the raft and were now standing up around the car. A man was leaning over the passenger window, where Chen sat. "Hey! Leave her alone!" Jordan screamed. He could hear Chong's yipping from here.

"They were planning to take your car all along," James said.

Jordan clenched his fists around the oars, feeling like an idiot. *Of course, they had been,* he thought.

"For what it's worth, it was brave of you to rescue all of us the way you did," Luke added.

Jordan barked a laugh. "Brave, sure. And stupid as hell." The adrenaline was making him feel dizzy. He looked back to his mom. Someone was trying to open the driver's side door, but his mom must've locked it because the door wouldn't budge. "Good girl, Mom," he muttered. "Hey!" he yelled again. "Stay away from her! I saved you, assholes! Now you stay away from her!"

They ignored him; not one looked in his direction. The man had something in his hand now. He started beating it against the car window. Jordan rowed until his arms felt like they were on fire. Luke and James each leaned to a side and tried to paddle with their hands to help speed things along. Chen's scream filled the air. "No!" Jordan yelled.

They were pulling her out of the car by her feet, yanking her through the driver's side. "She's just an old woman! Leave her, you fucks!" When they had her out, they let her fall to the water. With the snowmelt, it was still ice cold and she could go hypothermic in seconds, especially in her condition. The man reached back inside for Chong.

Chong was a ball of fury, twisting, growling, and biting in the man's hands. The man dropped him into the water next to Chen, who wasn't moving, while the others piled into the car. Jordan was still nearly a hundred yards away, fighting the current. He fought the tears that threatened to spill as he watched his mother helplessly.

"I'm coming, Mom!" he yelled.

LUKE AND JAMES LOOKED AT EACH OTHER, BOTH WITH PITY and fear in their eyes. They didn't know what else they could do, other than try to help move the kayak along faster. They had both tried to stop the others, tried to talk them down from the idea as soon as it was uttered. They were lucky to have been left on the rooftop and not dropped off the other side of the building.

LATER, WHEN THEY WERE CLOSE ENOUGH TO GET OUT AND walk, Jordan jumped from the kayak and ran through the water to his mother, who was still on her back. Her nose barely stuck up from the water; she was lucky to be breathing. Chong was on her stomach, shivering.

"I'm here," Jordan said. He scooped Chong into his sweatshirt, bundling him like a baby who needed his warmth.

The boys held on to the boat as Jordan held his mother's hand in his. She was still breathing, but it was shallow. "Mom?" He held her head in his arms and stroked her hair out of her face.

Chen coughed. "Jordy, I lost the car."

"No, you didn't lose it. I saw what happened. This is *not* your fault, Mom." Jordan couldn't fight his tears any longer. "I'm so sorry I wasn't here to protect you. How badly are you hurt? Can you move?"

"I think it's my back. Something happened. I can't feel anything."

Jordan clenched his fists. He closed his eyes and leaned his face up to the sky, letting the ash fall freely onto his skin. What was he supposed to do? He knew he wasn't supposed to move someone with a back injury, it could make it worse. He shouldn't even be holding her head, but he had to get her above the water. He checked his cell phone. No signal. There was no one around to help, no ambulances, no car to get to the hospital.

"We have to get you out of this water first, then we'll figure it out. You'll freeze if you stay here like this."

He took his sweatshirt off to give her a little support under her head, allowing him to stand up with Chong. He was about to ask Luke and James for some help. There was nothing else for it. She had to move. They would just have to be careful with her. Chen spoke again, stopping him. "No, Jordy."

"What do you mean?"

"Do you remember what your father said to you when you dropped out of school? About responsibility?"

"What? Mom, that was years ago. Why even bring that up—"

"He was right. You do have a responsibility. You're a good man, son. You help those who need you."

"I can't listen to this." He shook his head. "Hey guys—"

"It's too bad." She coughed again. This time blood came up, splattering onto her chin.

"Whoa!" Jordan bent back down to her, trying to take a closer look at her head and back without moving her. The water around her was turning red. "You're hurt!" he cried. Then he realized it was a stupid thing to say. Of course she was hurt. But she was hurt worse than he'd originally thought. He looked down at himself. Her blood was on him too.

"I love you, son," Chen said for the third time that day.

"Wait a minute, Mom. Give me a chance to move you. You're not dying. This is crazy." His words were rushed. He struggled against the panic that rose in his chest. He couldn't believe this was happening. Not now. First his dad and now this. It was too much to bear.

"Hey guys! I need your help, please," Jordan called. Luke and James pulled the kayak until they knew it was too shallow to float away. They rushed over, knowing it couldn't be good.

By the time they reached his side, Chen's hand had gone limp. A final breath left her lips. Jordan stared at his mother, disbelieving. He watched the ash piling on top of her body like snow in winter. It was quiet now; even Chong was silent. The only sound Jordan heard was the blood rushing in his ears.

He couldn't stop staring at her. A small part of him thought there was a chance she was just taking a nap. *How could this have happened so fast?* he asked himself. He felt dizzy. His head swayed. *Am I going insane?* he wondered. How could *both* his parents have died within hours of each other?

James cleared his throat. "Sorry, man."

"Yeah, sorry," Luke added. They both stood at a respectable distance, ready to help Jordan move his mother when he was ready.

Jordan was still holding her hand. Now that there was no risk of doing any further damage, he reached for her shoulder to lean her up. The back of her head was caved in. Blood was still oozing from it, and he could see her tissue as clear as day. The bastard had smashed her head in before yanking her from the car. He knew what he was doing.

Jordan sobbed openly, bending over his mother's body. He felt like his whole world was caving in. The regret and anger weighed on him heavier than he'd ever felt anything in his life. His soul felt like it was being crushed into nothing. "I'm so sorry," he whispered in her ear.

He was hyperventilating, gasping for air. Jordan felt like a kid again, one who'd been beaten up on the playground while the grownups weren't looking. He was desperate for his mom's comfort, only she couldn't provide it. She was *dead.* There was no one to help. He was alone now.

"I wanted to make you proud," he whispered between

gasps. He didn't know how he'd ever be able to live with himself. The guilt would devour him until there was nothing left but an empty husk.

Chong rustled in his arm, reminding Jordan he *wasn't* alone. Jordan stroked the dog's fur, taking comfort in a creature that loved both of his parents. He looked at Chong with new eyes. *I can still make her proud,* he thought.

Jordan took a steadying breath and wiped his eyes. He cleared his throat then said, "I can't leave her here like this."

"We'll help you put her someplace safe," Luke said.

"Thank you," Jordan whispered.

"We should probably find you a new sweatshirt too."

The three of them walked toward the sporting goods store to see what they could find.

CHAPTER
TWENTY-THREE

The wind shield wipers on Teresa's car were having a hard time keeping up with the ashfall. It reminded her of driving through the snow with the white flakes covering everything.

"Where are you taking me?" she muttered to herself, still following the man in the truck.

He was supposed to be leading her toward Pacific Avenue so she could cut over to Puyallup, but nothing around her looked familiar. He was leading her through the back roads, in the opposite direction of traffic, which is what she wanted, but it seemed like he was taking her in the wrong direction. *Maybe that's his tactic,* she thought. It made sense. He was probably trying to bypass everyone first, then cut over later. Maybe Pacific Avenue would still have too much traffic and that's why he was using different roads.

The ash seemed to get thicker the farther she drove. "Are we getting closer to Rainier?" The sun was setting now, and Teresa was beginning to worry. She'd wanted to get Luke and get the hell out of this state, but it now seemed that wasn't going to happen as quickly as she'd hoped. She was going to be lucky to find him at all.

"Hey!" Teresa called out the window. She turned on her

hazard lights and waved her arms, hoping the man would notice and pull over. It worked. He pulled to the side and waved her up to meet him. Turning off the car first, Teresa rolled down her passenger side window to talk to him.

"What's wrong?" he yelled across, impatient.

"Where are we going?"

"Aren't you listening to the radio?" He looked at her like she was stupid.

"Um, no. I don't understand. Is that supposed to tell me *where we're going?*" Being spoken to like that was one of Teresa's biggest pet peeves. She had enough people treating her that way on the phone, all day at work, she didn't need it now, too.

The man looked over to his passenger seat and said something to the person sitting next to him. He was too high up for Teresa to see who it was. After a few seconds, the man turned back. "We're not going anywhere," he said. "We're cut off and the only thing left to do is hunker down until the government gets their heads out of their asses and figures out how to get us out of here."

Teresa's eyes went wide. "What?"

"Which part of that did you not get?"

She scowled. This guy had seemed so helpful back in town. Now he just seemed like a dick. She looked around, noticing now that they were somehow the only ones on the road. *How is that even possible?* she wondered. "I need to get to my son," she said.

"Not my problem, lady."

"Okay, well can you tell me where we're headed? You've been leading me somewhere, haven't you?"

There was a tap on her driver's side window. Teresa's head jerked around to see another man standing there, smiling at her. Her palms began to sweat as it dawned on her this was not a good situation. Seeing the second man standing there, grinning at her like that, sent her heart rate into overdrive. She looked back from one man to the other.

"What is it?" she asked without rolling down her driver's side window.

He tapped on the window again, this time with the edge of a knife. "Open up."

"Why? No. I'm sorry, I've got to go." Teresa didn't wait to hear his response. She knew he wasn't there to chat. She started the car, ready to turn around and head back the way she'd come. But as soon as she started hers, the other man started his. Without warning, he pulled his lifted diesel forward, blocking Teresa's path forward.

"What the hell?" she cried. She shifted to reverse, ready to back up.

The man who'd been standing next to her window, was now behind her car, with both hands on her trunk.

"You think I won't hit you, asshole?" Teresa screamed. She held one foot on the brake, and with the other, hit the gas. Smoke blew out her exhaust into the man's face. His eyes bulged, surprised at her reaction. He jumped back, no longer confident that she wouldn't run him down.

The opening she needed was there. Teresa floored her car in reverse then turned it around. It took nothing for the man in the truck to block her a second time. This time, she couldn't back up. And she was no longer centered on the road, but off to the side, with a pine tree in back.

Black smoke billowed out of his tailpipes, filling the air with the smell of his diesel exhaust. Teresa felt the world closing in. "Let me go!" she yelled. She could no longer see the man standing on the road. "I can't believe this is happening," she whispered.

Seconds passed and then minutes, without movement. *Is this a stalemate?* she wondered, knowing it couldn't be. She was trapped like a mouse with its tail between a cat's paws. *What are they waiting for?* she wondered.

Teresa thought about making a run for it. Yes, they had the truck, but if she went into the trees, they'd have to get on foot too and she had a feeling she would be faster. *Unless they knew where they were going.* She gripped the steering wheel in both hands, closing her eyes, trying to decide what to do.

When her next breath came, her passenger window shattered. There were two men outside now, and one had smashed a bat against her car. Teresa screamed. As she ducked her head, her foot pressed down on the gas, in a knee-jerk reaction. Her car plowed into the side of the truck. It took everyone by surprise, including Teresa.

She was the quickest to recover. Moving the airbag out of the way, she reached to back up again. When one of the men outside dared to step in her path, Teresa kept the gas pedal floored. His screams came when she crushed his legs, but she didn't let up. "Fuck you!" she screamed, brave enough to let out a breath.

Teresa watched through the rearview mirror as the men helped their friend to the truck. She fought back the nausea and guilt when she caught a glimpse of the man she'd injured. "I hope that teaches them a lesson," she said, looking ahead again. She drove, not knowing where she was, and not caring. She was glad to be alive.

When Teresa looked back again, the truck was behind her once more. It was almost invisible this time, with no lights on in the fading light, with the white ash camouflaging it.

"Not again!" she cried, pressing the accelerator harder.

It wasn't enough. Within a few more minutes, the diesel truck overtook Teresa's sedan. The driver pushed into her once, hard enough to send her into the ditch.

A HAND WAS REACHING THROUGH THE FRONT PASSENGER window, grabbing for her. Teresa screamed, pressing herself against her driver's door, as far away as possible. With nothing else to defend herself, she clawed at the hand, hitting it, and scratching it. "Leave me alone!" she wailed.

"Come here, bitch. Don't make this harder than it has to be!"

The sound of another car approaching made them both turn their heads. Teresa didn't know what it was, but this one sounded even louder than the diesel truck. The man's hand pulled back. He ran away, back to his truck.

Teresa wiped the blood from her eyes, trying to get a clear view of what was happening. "Shit!" she said, trying to open the driver's door. It was stuck against the side of the ditch, unable to open. She thought about climbing through the passenger window, but also thought they were probably there waiting for her.

Full of fear and desperation, Teresa cried, afraid for her life, and more afraid of never seeing Luke again. Minutes passed and the oncoming car stopped. She could hear men talking but couldn't make out what they were saying.

There were a few of them. She wasn't sure how many. A dog barked. *A dog?* Now was the time to go. They were distracted by something, and it was now or never.

Teresa pulled herself toward the broken window. She climbed out, slicing her palms as she did. She winced at the pain but kept going until she was finally through. Staying as low as possible, Teresa kept inside the ditch, heading away from the men.

A gunshot rang out. She stopped moving. Teresa held her

breath, waiting, praying. The diesel truck started up. There was more yelling. Then the truck drove away.

"Hey, are you okay?" a man was yelling in the distance. He didn't sound like one of the men from the truck, but she couldn't tell for sure. It could be whoever was in the other car, but it could also be a trap.

"My name is Tim," the man said. "I just shot my gun."

Silence.

"I just want to make sure you're not hurt."

Teresa stayed quiet, still.

"Okay, well, I'm taking off now. Stay safe out here." His voice faded. She heard, "Come on, kid," as he seemed to get farther away.

If this was legitimate help and she let him leave, she'd be all alone in the dark. The other men could come back any time, and probably would. She would never make it on her own. There was no other choice. Her decision was made.

"Forgive me, Luke. If this is a mistake, I'm sorry, baby," Teresa whispered to herself, standing up. "I'm here," she said.

Tim turned around. "Are you alright?"

"They—" She shuddered. "They were trying to take me with them."

Tim nodded. "Taken care of."

"You scared them off? That's hard to believe."

"I'm sure you have an idea of what they had planned. When we stopped to see what all the fuss was about, it didn't take much for me to see what was going on. I'm glad I had Nate stay in the car." He nodded toward a boy that was next to him. "I don't know why they didn't have guns. I thought for sure they would." He shook his head. "I thought we were all goners. But turns out I was wrong. And we were all lucky that this little thing"—he held up his revolver—"did the trick. For now, at least."

Teresa nodded. She couldn't believe they didn't have guns

either. If she would've had a gun, she would've used it to scare them too and might not have been so nice about it.

"Now, are we gonna get out of here before they decide to come back?" Tim asked.

Teresa nodded again. She limped over to the black car that was still idling in the middle of the road.

"Squeeze in, and hang on. We don't go slow in this beauty." He smiled when Teresa looked at him and she knew from the look in his eyes that it wasn't a mistake to trust him.

CHAPTER TWENTY-FOUR

Tim drove them toward Seattle as the world turned dark. They sat in silence, the only sound that filled their ears was that of the engine roaring. Tim was too consumed with thoughts of what could've happened, what almost did happen, and Teresa too absorbed with thoughts about if she was making the wrong decision.

"I need to find my son," Teresa finally said.

"Okay. Where is he?" Tim had to practically yell for her to hear him over the car.

Teresa frowned. "I'm not sure. He was at school today and a friend was supposed to pick him up after the eruption, but I don't know if she did. He could still be at the school waiting for me, or he could've left on his own. I have no idea." Her lip quivered as she tried not to cry again.

"Hey it's okay." Tim glanced at her then back at the road. "I'm sure there's some kind of base camp already set up for survivors and everyone to find loved ones. We just have to figure out where it is. I think it could be in Seattle, which is the direction we're headed."

Survivors. Teresa wanted to weep just hearing the word. "Wouldn't it be at the border or something?" she asked. They wanted everyone to evacuate. Why would base camp be in Seattle?

"I mean, Seattle is a central location and the US Geological Survey headquarters. I need to check in with them. If nothing else, they'll know what's going on. Know how I can help."

"You're a geologist?"

"Yeah. Volcanologist."

Teresa's eyes grew wide. "You're the man who tried to warn us!"

Tim shrugged. "Did a great job of it, didn't I?"

"If you wouldn't have tried, I would've had no clue, not even a hint of what was happening until it was too late. You tried, Tim. That's what matters."

Tim nodded, but stayed silent.

Teresa looked at Nate. "Where are your parents?"

"They're at work."

"Where's their work? Do they know you're safe?"

Nate shrugged. "They work in Seattle."

Teresa sighed. It looked like Seattle was where they needed to be, but not her. She needed to be where Luke was. What if he didn't know about the base camp? What if there wasn't one, or if there was, what if it wasn't in Seattle? She ground her teeth together, trying to decide the best move to make.

"Will you drop me off in Puyallup? It's on the way to Seattle, anyway. I'll make my way from there."

Tim glanced at her, surprised. "You want me to drop you off alone, in the dark? After what just happened?"

"I mean yeah. I need to find my son. He could be out there in the dark, too. I need to find him. I'll just head for his school first and then go from there."

"Why don't you just stick with us until we reach base camp? If he's not there, I'll help you find him."

Teresa turned to look out the window as she thought some more. She was so torn. All she could think about was finding her boy, but was she being stupid? To be alone in the dark, with no way to find him, what could she really do?

If Tim and maybe even some others helped her, she would find him a lot sooner. If he was in trouble, she would have help with her. All she had to do was wait a little longer.

"Will we go out tonight?" she asked.

Tim nodded. "You bet."

"Okay." Teresa sighed in resignation. He was right, she shouldn't be alone at dark. Not after what she'd already been through.

Relief flooded Tim's features. Teresa smiled to herself, despite her worry for Luke. They continued their journey in relative silence, the sound of the engine filling the space between them again.

IT WASN'T LONG BEFORE THEY REACHED THE STREETS OF Puyallup. In the dark, ash made the road nearly invisible. "How can you see anything?" Teresa asked, squinting through the windshield.

"I can't," Tim said. He smiled at the look she gave him. "Let me know if you want to drive."

"I'll drive!" Nate said.

They started to laugh but stopped when water hit the windows. Tim slammed on the brakes, bringing them to an abrupt stop. "What is it?" Teresa asked.

"I think the street might be flooded."

Even with the headlights, it was nearly impossible to see. Mounds, where vehicles and other objects sat in the road, stood covered under the white ash. There were no street-lights, no city lights of any kind, to help shine the way.

When Tim opened the car door to step out, water came up to his ankles. "Flooded," he said, grimacing.

"How can it be flooded? The river is too far away. Isn't it?"

"I'm not sure how else it would happen, but I have a good idea that a lahar from Rainier could've caused it to overflow. I'll take a look around."

Tim closed the door to the car and used the light on his phone to shine his way. He didn't get far before he realized that the whole road was flooded. "It's flooded, alright," he said, coming back to the car. "I'm not sure if it's just here or the whole city, but it doesn't look good."

"Oh my God," Teresa said, feeling her heartbeat in her throat. She imagined Luke's school, her home, Naomi's house, all flooded. Anywhere Luke might be.

"I know you don't want to hear this," Tim said. "But maybe it gives him more of a reason to go to the base camp. Where else would there be to go? I bet we have a good chance of finding him there."

Teresa threw up her arms. "What if he doesn't know about the goddamn base camp? What if he's hurt somewhere, trapped and needing my help?" She shook her head. "Home is right here. This is our city. I have to look."

"Think about what you're saying for a minute. I know you're upset, but just listen to yourself."

Teresa was silent, glaring at Tim.

He pointed to Nate. "This kid has got to get to his parents. You are a parent, trying to get to your kid. You know how he feels."

Teresa looked at Nate who wouldn't meet either of their gazes.

"We have an obligation to get him to safety," Tim continued. "I *know* you need to find your son, but if you go out there alone in the dark, what are your real chances of finding him?"

Teresa clenched her jaw. She didn't want to hear all this again. They'd been over it all before. It was like beating a dead horse.

"So, what are we supposed to do? How do we get to Seattle?" Teresa wiped the cold sweat from her brow. She *had* to reach Luke. The image of him being hurt at school, all the different things that he could be suffering through, wouldn't stop flashing through her mind.

How was she supposed to find him now? She imagined her ten-year-old son alone in a flooded city, full of panicked people. Where would he go in the dark? Who would help keep him warm? Was he with Naomi or did she not make it to him? Teresa shivered thinking about it.

"It'll be okay," Tim said, recognizing the panic on her face. He turned her to face him. "There's still a base camp. We just have to find it."

"How are we supposed to do that? And how are you so sure there even is one?"

"It's a natural disaster. There's always a base camp. Since the roads are blocked to Seattle, my next best guess would be Tacoma. There's another US Geological Survey office there, and it's right next to the Narrows bridge, so some of the people who were trying to evacuate probably went that way anyway." His eyes lit up, warming more to the idea. "The port is right there too. It would be a great place to send supplies."

"Tacoma was a nightmare. I work there and I was barely able to make it out."

"It's either there, or Olympia and my bet would be on Tacoma."

"Olympia is the capital. Are you sure that wouldn't be a better guess?"

Tim thought for a moment, considering. Olympia was on

the way out of the state. People taking I-5 would be right there, trying to reach Oregon but there were so many other people, people who didn't make it that far, who would be affected by the eruption and who would need aid.

He had no way to know for sure, but he thought if he was a gambling man, Tacoma made more sense. There was an evac route that way, too, and all the government buildings. It would be more convenient for a base camp.

"It's your call," Tim finally said. "Worst case, we pick the wrong city, and it takes us longer to get there."

Teresa fought back the tears that wanted to spill. She couldn't afford to make the wrong choice. Who knew what would happen to Luke? He could be in trouble already. "I trust your judgment," she said. "Let's go to Tacoma."

CHAPTER TWENTY-FIVE

As they continued their journey toward Tacoma, it hit Teresa that they hadn't even tried the radio. The man in the diesel had said something about it, why hadn't she remembered? Everyone knew that's where emergency broadcasts were played, especially with the power being out. She reached for the radio dials, but nothing happened.

"The radio isn't working," she said.

"Yeah, I tried already. I don't think there's one installed."

Teresa leaned back in her seat. "Who builds a car with no radio?" She thought she'd probably die of boredom on her morning commute if she didn't have music to listen to.

Tim smiled knowingly. "I don't think they were using this as a commuter car. Besides, it's too loud for a radio."

Teresa could believe that one. She was starting to get a headache from the nonstop sound of the engine. "I can't imagine who would want a car this loud."

Tim laughed. "Lots of people, I'm sure. Car enthusiasts."

She looked back out the window, watching the night as they drove. Minutes passed until she spoke again. "I have to pee."

"Can you wait? We should be there soon."

"I've been holding it. I really need to go."

Nate spoke up. "I could go too. It's been a while."

"There's a Spendy Mart up the road." Teresa pointed at the billboard sign as they passed.

"Are you crazy?" Tim eyed her sideways. "You realize what's going to be going on at a Spendy Mart, right?"

"I know. I know. But they also have bathrooms, and I'm sure no one is going to be worried about the toilets when they can be taking everything else."

"It's dangerous. Even being around that kind of situation. People get attacked for no reason at all. They won't stop at the things the store has. They'll be looking for what *you* have too." Tim shook his head. "I don't think Nate should be in a situation like that."

Teresa sighed. "Do you see any other bathrooms around?"

"We can try—"

"I'll be fine," Nate said.

"No way." Tim shook his head. "I can't let you—"

"You're not my dad." Nate blushed. "I have to use the bathroom. Teresa is right. Spendy Mart is right there. You can stay and guard the car and we'll run inside really quick, do our business, and leave."

"Will someone please tell me what's wrong with finding a toilet at a house? We can knock on someone's door. There's bound to be people home!"

"Who's going to answer the door at a time like this?" Teresa asked.

Tim let out a soul-deep sigh. There was no time to argue about who was right or wrong, or if it was too dangerous—which he knew it was. If they had to go, they had to go. Tim turned toward the parking lot. "Okay," he said. "But I'm not guarding the damn car. I'm going with and I'll stand outside the stall if I need to."

FROM THE MOMENT THEY REACHED THE PARKING LOT, TERESA knew Tim was right. *I should've known better,* she told herself, unwilling to say the words out loud. It was too late now. She eyed Nate, hating herself for not listening to Tim, wondering how they were going to make it inside without anything bad happening. Wondering how they were going to do it with a *dog*.

"Are you sure you can't hold it?" she asked.

He was watching the people outside, too distracted to answer.

"Nate?"

He looked at Teresa with wide eyes. "Yeah?"

"Are you sure you can't hold it?"

HE GULPED. THE PEOPLE IN THE PARKING LOT WEREN'T *normal.* Not like anything he'd ever seen in his life. They were running in all directions, screaming, beating each other, carrying things out of the store, and then running back for more. People had trailers lined up outside the doors, being packed with TVs and other electronics.

Nate jumped as a gun went off. He felt like he was going to pee himself. Normally, he would just stand by a tree and do his business, but it wasn't pee he was worried about. The pressure was building. "I'm sure," he said weakly.

Teresa looked at Tim. "Let's be quick."

Tim looked angry. Not at them, but at the situation.

"Where are the police?" he asked, not really expecting an answer.

"They're spread so thin as it is. With no dispatch, I can't imagine what they're going through."

"You think the phone lines ever came back up?"

Teresa checked her phone. "Cell phones are still out. Landlines probably are too. They have their radios but that's probably it."

THERE WERE NO MORE PARKING SPACES. NOT LIKE NORMAL. Cars were packed in at every angle, as close to the doors as they could get. Some were trapped between others, with no way to back out or pull forward. Drivers parked in every position imaginable, some even on top of the flower beds.

Tim left the car toward the back, where he thought they'd have a better chance of getting out. It seemed everyone wanted to be as close to the doors as possible, so he thought they'd be safe enough farther back.

"Hold my hand, Nate," Teresa said.

He did without complaint, looking slightly relieved.

She looked at Tim. "Should we go to the bathrooms up front or in back?"

"Front. Electronics are in back."

"Shouldn't it be picked over by now? What about the money in the registers?"

Tim shook his head. "I don't think they keep money in them. Better stick to the front. And stay close."

Teresa grabbed his arm and the three of them walked in together. They had no leash for the dog, but he stayed by their side without wandering. Once inside, they hurried for the front bathrooms. Tears sprang to her eyes with the sight of the store. She wanted to cover Nate's eyes, would have if it was Luke with her. The thought made the tears fall.

"I can't believe this," she whispered.

People were swinging bats around, breaking anything they could reach. There were some ripping up clothing just for the hell of it. Others were piling anything they could get their hands on into cart after cart. Random things that didn't even matter—cheap jewelry, backpacks, thanksgiving decorations.

Some teenagers were running down the main aisle, screaming, chasing each other with clearance Halloween masks. Someone was driving a motorized scooter, running into anyone who wasn't paying attention. Most of the people were trying to grab anything that wasn't screwed down.

"Guess they didn't get the memo about the registers," Tim said as they passed. Someone had broken into all the front registers. They had either been empty, like he suspected, or every last cent had been taken. There was no trace of money left behind.

They finally reached the bathrooms. "Let's go in the men's," Tim said.

They listened without question.

Teresa and Nate each took a stall. Tim stood with his hand on the revolver. They were the only ones in the bathroom, so he locked the main door. The seconds ticked by.

"I'm too nervous," Nate said.

"Try to relax," Tim said, holding the revolver tight to his chest. He looked down at the dog, who was panting. "You want some water?"

Tim went to the sink to cup some water in his hands. He was busy watching the dog lap it up when the door rattled. The dog stopped drinking. They all held their breaths as muffled voices came from outside the door.

The door stopped shaking. The voices faded. Teresa tiptoed out of the stall without flushing. "Nate?" she whispered next to his stall door.

"I'm trying," he whispered back. It sounded like he was on the verge of crying.

Teresa and Tim met each other's knowing gazes. Time was short. They had to get the hell out.

"Do you think—" Teresa started in barely a whisper.

"What?"

"We could look for a radio. Just a small one. To see if there's a broadcast."

Tim shook his head. "Not worth it. Did you see what was going on out there?"

She frowned. "I guess you're right. You were right before."

Tim said nothing, too worried that someone was at the door listening. He petted the dog, trying to keep him as quiet as possible. Nate was taking forever. When he flushed the toilet, it was like a bolt of electricity shot through each of them.

They stood frozen, staring at Nate as he walked through the stall door. He started crying. "I'm sorry. I forgot."

They waited for a noise to come at the door again. A minute passed, and then two. The dog whimpered.

"Let's get out of here," Tim finally said.

CHAPTER TWENTY-SIX

They walked out together, the same as they'd walked in. A sense of disbelief filled Teresa. She couldn't register that nothing had gone wrong. No one had said a word to them. Just the little rattle at the bathroom door. Something didn't feel right about it. It was too *easy*.

"Hey! Nice dog!" a man sneered at them.

Teresa wanted to kick herself for thinking anything that might've jinxed them.

"Keep walking," Tim said to her.

They walked faster through the parking lot, ignoring the man.

"Here doggy," the man taunted, following them.

The dog's ears perked up. He slowed down, thinking the man wanted to pet him.

"No, boy," Nate said. He took hold of the dog's fur and gently tugged him forward.

"Hey!" the man yelled. "Too fucking good to let me pet your dog?"

"He's not going away," Teresa whispered.

"Just get to the car. We're almost there," Tim whispered back.

Teresa tightened her grip on Nate's hand. He didn't seem

to mind her sweaty palms. There were more footsteps behind them and then more voices.

"Hey, where ya going?"

"Hey, don't walk away from us, assholes!"

Teresa felt like she might faint. She saw Tim gripping the gun with his other hand. What were they going to do if the people behind them had a gun too? She wanted to yell at them to go away but was afraid that would only piss them off.

Tim wasn't a small guy, he looked like he could hold his own. But Teresa didn't know if she could. And she didn't think Nate could, either. He was just a kid. She chanced a glance behind, to see three people still following. *There might be more,* she thought.

"Here, doggy, doggy."

"Hey, got any food?"

"Are you hungry again? God, you're fat."

"What? I haven't eaten since lunch."

"You just had that bag of chips inside."

"That was just a snack."

As they argued among themselves, Teresa picked up her pace, tugging Tim and Nate with her. The dog seemed to get the hint too. They weaved between cars, trying to get ahead as much as possible.

They gained a little space, but not much. "Where's the car?" Teresa asked between clenched teeth.

"I think we're farther back," Tim said.

It was hard enough trying to find it through the mess of cars, but with no lights, it was harder than they imagined. "Is that it?" Nate asked. He was too afraid to point, in case the people following saw.

"Where?" Teresa asked.

"Ahead. To the left."

"I don't see it."

"Nate, head that way," Tim said.

Relief filled them all when the car came into sight. It was only a few feet away now. Then the car's lights came on. Teresa couldn't stop the guttural scream that came when their car started without them in it.

Laughter came behind them. The others were still following. Tim ran for the car, but it was too late. He tried to yank the door handle open, but it was locked. He pounded on the window. "That's not your car!" he screamed.

Whoever was in the driver's seat revved the engine.

"Use your gun!" Teresa yelled. "Break the glass!"

Tim slapped the revolver against the window. After one hit, the driver floored the car in reverse, causing Tim to fall forward. Teresa screamed again when the car pulled forward, headed straight for Tim.

The car swerved at the last minute, passing them and speeding away. They didn't have time to catch their breath before the people behind caught up. "What do we do now?" Teresa asked.

"I don't understand how they could start it," Tim said. "I have the keys right here." He held them up to show her.

"It doesn't matter." Teresa looked behind them again. The people would be on them in two seconds. She grabbed Nate and started walking. "Come on, Tim. We have to get out of here."

STILL DAZED AND CONFUSED, TIM STARED AFTER THE CAR'S taillights. "I just don't understand."

"Sorry about your ride, man," someone said.

Tim looked over to see the group that finally caught up.

He clenched his jaw, fed up with this night already. "What's wrong with you?" he asked. "The volcano erupts, and you think it's the end of the world? You think you can do whatever the hell you want?"

The man held a hand under his chin, as if in deep thought. "Hmm. Yeah, that about sums it up." He grinned.

"I don't think so."

Tim pointed his gun at the man. The others with him stopped advancing. "Stop following us. Leave us alone."

The man laughed. "What are you gonna do about it?"

The blast from the gun was earsplitting. The man dropped to the ground, along with his friends. "The next one won't go in the air," Tim said. "Now, are you going to leave us the hell alone?"

They all nodded their agreement.

"Now I'm going to walk away. If one of you follows again, I'm not going to give a warning shot."

Tim turned around and ran before they got the nerve to jump him and steal his gun. He caught up with Teresa and Nate, who were hiding behind a car waiting for him with the dog. "I'm sorry," Tim said. "I'm so sorry."

Teresa held his arm. "It's not your fault. None of this is your fault."

"I don't see how it's not."

"I don't see how it is," she said. "Now, we're close, or at least we should be. Let's walk."

PART
THREE

CHAPTER TWENTY-SEVEN

Rick looked at the back of his hands. His knuckles were turning white from gripping the steering wheel so tight. He grimaced in disgust. The old woman's blood was on him. He wanted to wipe it off, but then it would be on his clothes. His elbow shoved forward, causing the steering wheel to jerk to the left. "Move over, fat ass!" he yelled.

"I'm sorry, it's crowded as fuck in here," Jose said.

"You can come sit by me," Felicity said from the back seat. She wiggled her eyebrows suggestively, making Jose blush.

"Knock it off. I don't want to see that shit. When we get to The Farm, you guys can have as much ass as you want," Rick said, elbowing Jose in the side.

"Hey, you think Gary and them picked anyone up? This is the perfect day to do some business." Jose rubbed his hands together, imagining the payday that would come. In a situation like this, with everyone panicked, no one knowing who *not* to trust. The sheep practically walk right into their hands.

"I'm sure they got some," Rick said. He slammed his palm on the steering wheel, making the others jump. "We could've had those kids."

"No way, man," Kevin chimed in from the back seat. "I

mean, look at us. We're packed in here like fucking sardines. How the hell were we supposed to get anyone else in this ride? And besides, you know they woulda squealed. It's why we left them there." He shook his head. "Nah, I'm glad we didn't get them."

"I don't give a fuck if you're glad, Kevin," Rick said. "If that old bitch wouldn't've put up a fight, we could've had the ride *and* the kids. We could've left her there *alive* and took the others with. It would've worked out fine. But that old woman…"

"But what about the other guy? The one who was with her?" Jose asked.

Rick was silent. It didn't matter now. They had the ride. They left the goods behind. Nothing for it. Gary would understand. Besides, he was sure plenty of others would come their way. They always did. And like Jose said, this was the perfect situation for it.

The Farm, as everyone called it, was a fifty-acre piece of property that Gary owned out in the middle of nowhere. Most of the property was forested and private. He wanted it that way for a reason.

As soon as Rick pulled up to The Farm, everyone piled out. They stretched their arms, legs, and backs, all groaning from being cramped for so long. Rick wanted to yell at them to quit complaining. They were lucky some idiot had come along to get them off the rooftop to begin with, but he wasn't in the mood. He left them to their own devices while he went to find Gary.

"Please tell me you got somethin'," Gary said when Rick walked into the house.

Rick flinched when the screen door slammed behind him. He walked across the old wood floor that creaked with each step he took. When he finally got to Gary at the kitchen table, he wasn't sure what to say. In the car, he'd thought for sure that Gary would understand, but now, seeing the look in his eyes, Rick wasn't quite so sure anymore.

"We had some problems," Rick said.

"Oh, yeah? So sorry to hear that, Ricky." Sarcasm from Gary wasn't a good sign. And it *really* wasn't good when Gary called him Ricky.

Rick tried not to wince. "The whole fucking city flooded. We were stuck on a roof for hours until some asshole got us down. That's the only way we even had a ride out of there."

Gary nodded. "So, some shmuck saves you, gives you his car out of the kindness of his heart, and somehow you *still* weren't able to bring anything back to me?"

Rick cleared his throat. "It's not that simple."

"Oh, isn't it?"

"Nah. I mean, there was an old woman I had to handle. These kids almost gave us away. It was a headache, Gary, trust me."

"Trust you?" Gary stood up. A second later, he was laughing so hard he had to wipe tears from his eyes. "Fuck Rick, you should see the look on your face!" He doubled over, holding his side.

Rick smiled. "Thanks for bustin' my balls, man."

Gary grinned. "That's my job, ain't it?" Once he composed himself, he said, "I know it's a shit show out there. I almost had this little beauty too, but she put up a fight. She ran right over Eric's legs."

Rick's eyes grew wide. "She what?"

"Yeah. Don't think I'm about to let that one go either. If I ever come across her again, you bet your ass payback is mine. Point is, I'm not holding it against you for not bringing any goods back today. And," Gary nodded toward the stereo sitting on the table. "It looks like we're gonna have a little change in plans anyway."

"You name it, I'm down."

Gary smiled. "That's my boy."

"So, what happened?"

"I was out in Tacoma when the freeway closed. Traffic was sure a bitch today." He laughed. "Anyway, it worked out fine for me. At first, anyway. There was this woman who walked straight into my lap. She was looking for a way through, anyway I told her to follow me. I almost had her out here, but she must've caught on somehow. We ran her off the road and long story short, some knight in shining armor came to her rescue."

"Nosy bastard," Rick said.

"Yeah. Tell me about it. But we were stupid, underestimated her. Underestimated him too. It won't happen again."

Rick nodded. It'd happened to him today, too.

CHAPTER
TWENTY-EIGHT

The others started gathering inside the house, crowding around Gary and Rick, who were listening to the radio. It was clear how concentrated Gary was on the words being broadcast. No one made a sound.

"This is an emergency broadcast message. This is not a drill. I repeat, this is not a drill. If you can hear this message, please stay tuned." The message repeated, followed by static.

"Turn that shit up," Gary said. His brows furrowed as he tried to make out what was being said through the crackling.

"It's just static," Felicity said, not wanting to get up from Jose's lap.

As soon as her words were out, Jose's eyes grew wide. "She didn't mean it, boss." Giving her a pointed look, Jose pushed her off his lap so he could stand up to reach the radio.

"What's the big deal?" Felicity whispered in his ear. She was new to the group and didn't fully understand the consequences of questioning the boss. No one dared disobey him, no matter how small his request. It wasn't something Jose had seen done before and he was pretty sure no one would make the mistake twice.

Jose's efforts to save Felicity were too late. Now that she was off his lap, she was close enough for Gary to reach his arm out and grab her. With seemingly no effort, he grasped a fistful of her hair and yanked her down to his seated level. She cried out in surprise, and tears sprang to her eyes from the sudden pain.

Gary wrapped her long black hair around his fist, pulling harder. "I don't recall *asking* for your opinion," he said, staring into Felicity's eyes.

"I-I—"

"Shut up."

Keeping her in his grip, Gary turned his attention back to the radio. Everyone in the room was silent, afraid to even breathe too loudly.

"This is a message from the United States Armed Forces. It has been approximately twelve hours since Mount Rainier erupted, isolating a large portion of Western Washington and preventing residents from evacuating. We are well aware that those individuals who are still trapped are quickly running out of food and other supplies. Emergency supplies are being flown in and will be distributed fairly and evenly. Military personnel are out helping those who are trapped. If you are in need of supplies, and able to, please make your way to the Tacoma Dome. We will receive supplies within the next twenty-four hours and hand them out on a first-come, first-served basis. Please remain orderly and calm in these dire circumstances. Remember to be safe. Thank you."

The message started to repeat but no one wanted to speak before Gary. A smirk on his lips, he waited, enjoying the anxiety in their eyes. The only one who wasn't completely afraid was Rick, but that was okay. Rick was fine.

"Turn it off," Gary said, nodding to Jose.

Felicity let out a whimper as Gary adjusted his fingers in her hair. His hand was starting to sweat now but he wasn't through with her yet. "Now, it seems that good ole Jose hasn't informed you on the way things are done around here. Is that right, Jose?"

"I did, boss. I swear I did."

"Uh-huh, well that's good of you. Then, in that case, Felicity might just have a little hearing problem. Do you, dear?"

"D-do I what?"

"Have a hearing problem?" Gary screamed it in her ear, pinning her head down against the chair so she couldn't jerk back. Felicity squinted against the sound, unable to stop the tears from coming.

"No," she whispered.

"What's that?"

"No. I don't have a hearing problem," she said a little louder.

"Oh, good. It must be your memory then." Using the fist that was wrapped around her hair, Gary took Felicity's head and pounded it into the edge of the wooden table that they were all sitting around. There was a loud pop, and he wasn't sure if he'd split his table or her head, but hoped for the latter because the table was an heirloom.

Felicity cried out and Gary smashed her into the table again. "One more time, for good measure." He slammed her into the wood a third time before letting go. "Next time you have a memory problem, it'll be your last. I don't do second chances."

With blood running down her face, Felicity wobbled toward Jose. She tried to wipe some of the blood from running into her eyes but was too disoriented and wound up swatting her hair instead.

WHEN EVERYONE LEFT, IT WAS JUST GARY AND RICK IN THE room again. Rick sat in silence, thinking about the plan that Gary had just dished out to him. He twirled his beard hairs between his fingers, playing it out in his mind's eye.

"What's eating you?" Gary asked, watching him.

Rick shook his head. "Nothing. Just playin' out the plan in my head."

"You've been silent about it. It not good enough for you?"

Rick laughed. "It's a good plan, boss."

"Then what?"

Gary wasn't one to ask or care about others' opinions, but Rick was different. He was smart enough for Gary to trust his input a smidge more than everyone else. He was still too full of himself, but who wasn't?

"We're talking about the US military. The government. Big Brother. We've never dealt with anything like that before. I'm not sure I can trust some of the others to pull it off."

"You're doubting me?"

"No. Not you."

Gary's lips pressed together in a fine line. He didn't like what he was hearing out of Rick's mouth. "If you don't trust someone on the team, I need to know about it. This isn't a game. All our lives are at stake, even without this new plan. Traitors and the incompetent need to be dealt with."

"I didn't want to say anything until I had some concrete facts. I'd hate to accuse someone of something if it wasn't true."

"I'd rather you accuse someone falsely," Gary said. "At least then, we know there're no mistakes that matter."

Rick frowned. He nodded. "Got it."

"Well. Spill the fuckin' beans."

"Felicity. I'm not sure if she's playing the dumb bitch, or actually is one. I think it might be a front."

"And that means someone's on to us."

"I could be wrong."

Gary waved an arm. "She's undercover. Let's leave it at that. Question is… is she with the police or someone else? No. You know what? It doesn't matter."

"It doesn't?" That was news to Rick.

"Nope. We have friends in high places. How do you think we got advance warning about Rainier?"

Rick nodded. *That* he did know. "What if she's working for a so-called friend?"

Gary laughed. "I like how you think. Sure, it's possible, but I don't think so. Trust me on this one."

"Alright. I'll handle it."

CHAPTER
TWENTY-NINE

Teresa, Tim, and Nate walked until Nate looked like he'd fall asleep on his feet. They huddled against the November chill, breathing through their shirts to block the ash as much as possible. When they were so exhausted they could barely move, Tim found them a place to sleep.

"We should be fine here," he said.

Teresa wrapped her sweater tighter around herself. She looked around the abandoned alleyway and shook her head. "I don't know about this."

"Do you have any better ideas? This is the safest place we've found."

"I don't know how safe I feel here."

"Let's sleep in shifts then. You guys get some shut-eye and I'll keep watch. We'll trade off in a few hours."

Teresa glanced around again. Too tired to argue, she agreed to the plan. She wrapped herself behind Nate, who was already fast asleep on top of some cardboard with the dog. She brushed the hair out of his eyes and noticed something on the ground beside him.

"What's this?" Teresa held up what looked like a small pocketknife.

"Oh that," Tim said. "I forgot he had that. He took it from the gift shop when we were at the national park."

Teresa frowned, looking at it.

Tim shrugged.

She put it in her pocket. "Remind me to give it to him when he wakes up. Don't forget to wake me."

Tim smiled. "I won't."

TIM OPENED HIS EYES, MOMENTARILY CONFUSED BY HIS surroundings. Slumped over on a pile of pallets, he saw that he was in an alleyway. He blinked at all the ash, coughed, then it hit him. "Shit!"

Tim jumped up. "Teresa."

She and Nate were still asleep. The dog was gone. When neither moved, Tim shook Teresa's arm. "Hey, we have to wake up."

She jerked forward then stretched.

"What time is it?" Nate asked.

Tim checked his phone and grimaced. "It's nine."

"Nine? Oh my God, Tim!"

"I know, I'm sorry."

Teresa brushed the ash off herself as best she could. "Any cell service yet?"

"None."

"Where's the dog?" Nate asked, looking around. He started back down the alleyway.

"Hey, Nate, Let's stick together, okay?" Teresa called.

Nate ignored her, continuing his search. Teresa and Tim shared a look before hurrying after him. Back on the road,

Tim almost choked when he couldn't see Nate. "Where'd he go? He wasn't that far ahead of us."

"Nate!" they called together.

"Over here."

Teresa and Tim rushed toward Nate's voice. He was inside a parked car with the door open. When they reached him, they both breathed a sigh of relief. Nate and the dog were together, both safe and happily snacking on a bag of chips.

"Do you think you should be eating after the dog?" Teresa asked. She couldn't help but smile at the scene of Nate and the dog happily sharing their snack.

"I'm starving," Nate said between bites.

"Me too, kid," Tim said. "Want to share the wealth?" he asked with a laugh.

AFTER HOURS OF EXPOSURE, THEY WERE ALL READY TO BE inside. And they were finally getting close. "Look!" Nate cried, pointing at the parking lot of Tacoma Dome.

The hum of generators filled the air, powering what seemed like hundreds of lights. Tents were set up to cover people in line, all weighed down by ash that was still falling. The dog barked in response to Nate, eager to find out what his excitement was about.

"Looks like Tacoma was the right choice," Teresa said with a smile.

Tim smiled back at her. "It's going to be okay. Your son could be there already waiting for you."

"I hope you're right."

"Register your names here, please. The dog will have to be boarded outside. Food and shelter are inside the dome," a man instructed as soon as they approached base camp.

"Do I have to board the dog?" Nate asked. He looked like he might cry at the idea of leaving the dog behind.

"I'm sorry, it's for his own safety."

Nate looked at Tim. "Do we have to stay here?"

"Sorry, Nate. This is probably the safest place for us right now. And we need to help Teresa find her son. Your parents are probably looking for you too. They could be here."

"They're not."

"You don't know that for sure."

"I do."

Tim sighed. "Okay, well, let's look around a bit and try to help Teresa. Give it a little while and let's see what happens. I know you don't want to hear this, but the dog does have an owner. Don't get too attached, okay?"

Nate didn't look happy. He thought about it, then finally nodded. "Okay. For a while. He seemed to ignore the other part of what Tim said." Nate bent down to pet the dog, rubbing his back and behind his ears. He whispered, "I'll get you soon, boy."

Teresa felt terrible for Nate. "Maybe you can stay near him, while he's in the kennel. I'm sure they need volunteers to help with the animals."

Nate's eyes brightened at the idea. He looked at Teresa and then to the man checking them in.

The man looked concerned. "How old are you?"

"I'm twelve," Nate said.

"And where are your parents?"

"At work. They're not here. I'm fine. I just want to stay with the dog."

The man could clearly see the determination on Nate's face. There wasn't time to argue, and it was pointless. There were too many people who needed help and they could use every spare, able-bodied person who was willing to help, despite their age. If the kid was helping, he was close and safe. He finally said, "We can use all the help we can get. Thank you."

Nate's grin reached his eyes.

Tim said, "We're going to look for Teresa's son. We'll check in on you soon."

"What's his name?" the man asked.

"Luke Thomson," Teresa said.

He checked his system, then ruffled through some paperwork. "Doesn't look like he's checked in yet. It's possible he slipped by when we were first setting up, though."

Disappointment filled her. She couldn't speak, only nodded. She could only hope he would figure out to come here. She gave Nate a hug before walking through.

THERE WAS SO MUCH TIM NEEDED TO DO. SO MANY PEOPLE HE needed to speak with. He knew the US Geological Survey had to be set up at base camp, but right now, he was worried about keeping his promise to Teresa.

"You can do whatever you need to do," she said. "Thank you for getting me here—for saving my life. You don't owe me anything. You don't have to babysit me anymore."

Tim laughed. "Babysit you? I'm trying to help you. I made you a promise and I'm going to keep it."

"You don't have to. It's okay."

"Call me old school, but I consider myself a man of honor. If I make a promise, I keep it. And if I don't, I can't sleep at night. It's for me, as much as for you." He smiled. "Now, enough bickering. Where should we look first?"

Base camp extended through the parking lot and into the Tacoma Dome. The building itself spanned over six acres and already seemed full. "Maybe we should split up to cover more ground?" Teresa said.

"That would be a good idea, except I have no idea what he looks like."

She pulled out her phone to show him a picture of Luke. "Here, take my phone. There's still no signal anyway, so it's not like he's going to call me."

"Great. Let's meet back here, by the entrance, in say, an hour."

"Sounds good."

Teresa moved through the building with determination but little hope. The feeling in the pit of her stomach told her Luke wasn't there, but she was still going to look at as many faces as she could. She could be wrong. The man at the check-in could be wrong. She wasn't going to waste time twiddling her thumbs; she was going to *look*.

As she pushed her way through, her heart clenched at the sight that met her eyes. People were covered in ash from head to toe. Some were coughing so hard they were gasping for air. Others were wearing oxygen masks.

There were a few people who looked wet and muddy—probably got caught up in the landslide and were lucky to be alive. When she thought about it, they were all lucky to be alive. She made eye contact with an older woman whose husband was asleep beside her. The man lay on a cot, snoring with his mouth open. The woman looked miserable.

"Hi there," Teresa said. She gave a small smile. "I'm looking for my son. I was wondering—"

"Jim!" the woman yelled. She slapped the top of his stomach hard, making the man choke on his snore and flail his arms.

"What's going on?" he cried.

"Stop that damned racket. I'm trying to talk to this woman, and I can't hear a word she's saying over your snoring." She smiled back at Teresa. "I'm sorry, dear. Now what were you saying?"

Teresa glanced at the man, who was blushing furiously and looked like he'd like to murder his wife. He mumbled something to himself before making the battle to get up off the cot.

"Do you need help, sir?" Teresa asked.

He waved her off.

She waited until he was up and walked away before resuming her conversation with the woman. "I'm so sorry," she said. "I didn't mean to cause any trouble."

"Nonsense. He's always snoring so loud he could wake the damned dead. I was about to smack him anyway."

"I'm looking for my son. He was at school when this all went down, and I was at work. I'm not sure if he's alone or not but I was wondering if there's any chance you might've seen a ten-year-old who looks something like me."

Sympathy filled the woman's eyes. "I'm sorry, dear. To be honest, I haven't paid much attention. I can tell you I haven't seen any young boys who are alone, if that helps."

Teresa nodded. "It does a bit, thank you."

"Where are you from? What's his name?"

"Puyallup. His name is Luke. Mine is Teresa."

"It's nice to meet you, Teresa. I'm Charlotte, and that was my husband, Jim. We're from Orting."

"It's nice to meet you too, Charlotte. Thank you for your time." Teresa started to leave but Charlotte continued.

"I'll sure keep my eye out for Luke."

"I appreciate that. Good luck to you and your husband."

CHAPTER THIRTY

Teresa moved on, continuing her search. She was almost back around to the front of the building, ready to meet up with Tim again, when someone grabbed her shoulder. That simple touch rocketed hope through her. She felt like a bolt of electricity had shot through her from her heart to her limbs. Her eyes watered when she turned, thinking she'd see her son.

It wasn't Luke, though. It was Luke's best friend's mom, Naomi. Next to her was her son, Trevor. Tears fell. This was the moment she'd been waiting for. She was finally going to be reunited with her son, safe and sound. He was here. Her gut had been wrong. The man at the front check-in had been wrong. It was all over now.

"Teresa, I'm so sorry," Naomi said.

And just like that, Teresa's world came crashing down. She stumbled, losing her balance. If Luke wasn't with them, where was he? Who was he with? Was he alone? An image of the man who tried taking her flashed before her eyes. What if there was someone like that who'd tried to grab Luke too. What if they succeeded?

A small moan escaped Teresa's throat without her realizing it. She put a hand to her mouth. "Where is he?" she asked.

"I couldn't find him at the school. I was panicking. I'm so sorry. I found Trev and Luke wasn't with him and I just couldn't—" She wiped tears from her cheeks. "It was all chaos. The bleachers collapsed—"

"They what?"

"From the quaking, I guess. Hundreds of kids were trapped or crushed under them. I was so worried about Trevor. I needed to get him out of there." She looked at Teresa with pleading eyes, begging for understanding.

"Oh my God. Oh my God!" Teresa wanted to scream. *The woman on the phone had been right.* She felt light headed. She needed to do something with her hands to keep her from throttling Naomi's throat. She clenched and unclenched her fists. Teresa looked down at Trevor, who was crying too. "Do either of you have any idea if—" She swallowed. "If Luke was okay?"

Naomi shook her head, more tears streaming down her face.

"I heard him," Trevor said.

Teresa bent to his level. "Did he sound hurt? Did you see him?"

"I… we were on the lower level before the collapse. I don't think he went under, but I don't know for sure. I tried to find him. I called for him. He answered but he was in the crowd."

"I'm so sorry, Teresa," Naomi said again.

Teresa closed her eyes. She wanted to hate this woman. She wanted to blame her for everything. But she couldn't. When it came down to it, it wasn't Naomi's fault. Luke was *her* son, and she wasn't there for him.

"He could've been helping other kids," Trevor choked out.

It warmed Teresa's heart to hear the words. Trevor was right. Luke could've been helping and if he wasn't hurt, she'd bet her bottom dollar that it's exactly what he was doing. "You're a good friend, Trevor," she said.

Even though Teresa didn't fully blame Naomi, there was still a part of her that would never feel the same toward her again. Their friendship, no matter how small it was, was now over. Both women felt it. How could it ever be the same?

Teresa knew she should say something else. She should reassure Naomi that it wasn't her fault, tell her she didn't blame her. She couldn't say the words now, though. Maybe when she had Luke in her arms, and everything was okay again, maybe then she would tell Naomi. For now, she remained silent. All she could do was walk away.

When Teresa met back up with Tim, she was still crying. She was angrier than she'd ever been in her life. Angrier than Jerry or anyone else in her life had ever made her. She was furious with herself.

"What happened?" Tim asked, concern in his eyes. "What did you find out?"

Teresa shook her head. "The woman who was supposed to pick him up from school—I saw her." She was racked by more sobbing. Tim put an arm on her shoulder, trying to comfort her.

Teresa wiped the tears and snot away. "She never picked him up. She left him all alone."

Tim frowned. He didn't know what to say to that, wasn't sure that any words would matter anyway. He didn't have kids and could only imagine what Teresa must be going through. "He might show up on his own. Kids are resilient.

He could walk right through those doors and surprise the hell out of you."

"What if he doesn't? Am I just supposed to sit here and wait for him? What if he's hurt? She said the bleachers at school collapsed. He could've been trapped under there."

"There's no easy choice. Do what you think is best. We can go searching or we can wait. Either way, you're going to be wondering if you made the wrong decision."

Teresa grasped Tim's hand in hers. "Tim, it's been over twenty-four hours since I've seen my son. Luke isn't here. I can't stay." She let go of his hands to brush away the tears that were brimming her eyes. "I have to find him."

"I think you're right."

"You mean you're not going to try talking me out of leaving?"

"No. We said we'd look for him here and he's not here. Let's find your boy."

A stray tear fell unbidden. "Thank you," Teresa whispered. "Where do you think we should look first?"

Tim smiled. "I was hoping you would have an idea. Your son and all that."

She frowned. "He's probably on foot. He has to be." She looked up at Tim. "Unless he got a ride with someone else. Do you think he made it down to Oregon?"

"Do you think he would evacuate without you?"

"No." She shook her head. "I don't think he would. I think he would try to find me."

"Alright. Then let's work off that. He'd try to find you. He's on foot. Where's he headed?"

"Either to home or my work. That's it."

"No other friends he might check in with?"

"No. I don't have many who are that close." Her cheeks heated. "I'm sort of a workaholic."

"You said you work here in Tacoma, right?"

"Yeah."

"Perfect. Then with any luck, Luke will be close too."

Teresa looked away, unable to look into his eyes anymore. "I don't know what to do," she admitted.

"I can only imagine what you must be feeling," Tim said. "If it helps at all, waiting here might not be such a bad idea. I know I just said I wasn't going to try talking you out of it, and I'm not, but I just want you to look at it from another angle. You're safe, and he really could show up any minute. As soon as you leave, you have no way of knowing if he's going to show up when you're gone."

Teresa was silent for a moment. Her eyes were shimmering from unshed tears, and she was deep in thought. Finally, she nodded. "I'll give it a little while to see if he shows up."

"Alright. I need to speak with some people. Give me a heads-up when you're ready to set out and I'm there with you. Don't forget my promise."

"Take me with you. I want to be in the loop."

Tim thought about it. Then he shook his head. "I don't think it's a good idea. They fired me. It could get ugly, and I don't want to drag you into it."

"Maybe I can help."

"I appreciate it, but I won't be long. Keep your eye out for Luke. I'll be back before you know it. And here's your phone back."

Teresa took her phone before giving Tim a hug. "Thank you, Tim."

CHAPTER
THIRTY-ONE

"It's been a whole day," Luke said. "I can't believe we haven't found a car yet."

"We slept in one last night. What are you talking about?" Jordan said.

"I mean, we're still walking."

"People are too afraid to trust other people. I don't blame them. Look what happened to him." James nodded toward Jordan.

Luke grimaced. "Yeah, but with all the people running around, you would think we would find one parked somewhere, with the keys still in it."

"Sure. Probably right in the middle of the traffic jam. Good luck getting it out."

"Okay, well what about food then? Those vending machine snacks that Jordan had were fine for dinner, but we haven't eaten all day. You would think there would be something in one of these cars, or *somewhere*."

"Who's going to leave food lying around when there's no guarantee when they'll be able to go grocery shopping next?"

"You're just full of positivity today, aren't you?" Luke scowled.

James barked a laugh. "I'll be positive when something

positive actually happens. So far, this has been a shit show from hell. *Nothing* has gone right except you saving me from those bleachers."

Luke blushed. He didn't want to be considered a hero. He'd just done what he thought was right. He hoped he wasn't the only person out there who was like that. He *knew* he wasn't. Jordan was the perfect example.

They were silent again, walking through the crowded streets, following Jordan's lead. Each car they passed had people camped out inside, some looking frightened, some looking bored. Luke didn't understand how people could stay like that. They hadn't moved an inch in over a day. The only thing that made sense was that they didn't have to deal with the ash inside their cars.

"Why aren't more people at home? I don't understand," Luke said.

"They're afraid," Jordan answered. "Or the smoke and ash are getting in their houses, so it doesn't do much good staying home if that's the case."

"But it has to be better than being out here." A coughing fit hit Luke, causing him to stop walking. He held on to the car next to him for balance. It was so covered that he couldn't tell the type of vehicle, or even the color of it.

"Get your hands off my car!" someone yelled from inside.

When his coughing abated, Luke looked closer to see a woman's eyes peering at him through the window. He jerked back, alarmed at her hostility. "Sorry," he mumbled.

"Ignore her," Jordan said.

They continued on. Not everyone stayed inside their cars. There were some who took their families and abandoned their vehicles. The roads were flooded with people, trying to make it to what they considered safety. Jordan, Luke, and James weren't the only ones on foot. They also weren't the only ones who'd been robbed. Just like clockwork, every few minutes someone cried out for help to fight off others who wanted to take advantage of the circumstances.

"Jordan, where are we even going? Do we know?" James asked.

"I'm just sort of following the crowd, unless either of you has a better idea."

Luke and James looked at each other. "I have to find my mom," Luke said.

"Yeah, we've established that. But since we don't know where she is, and she's probably trying to find you… it might be best to stay with the crowd. Safety in numbers and all that."

Luke began to cough again.

"We need to get out of this ash. He's going to get sick if he's not already. We need to get inside," James said.

Jordan looked around. They could sit inside one of the abandoned cars, or they could try for an abandoned house. There were stores nearby but all had broken windows and looters running in and out. They weren't safe. "If we leave the crowd, we're going to have to face them again." He pointed to a group of looters breaking into a house up the street.

"I'll be fine," Luke said. His lungs felt like they were on fire, but he would push on. He wasn't going to be a baby and put Jordan and James in more danger. Why should they have to stop just for him?

"Hey man, it's okay. We'll stop," James said.

"I'm sure." Luke looked at Jordan. "Let's stay with the crowd. You're right. It's safer."

Jordan nodded.

THEY STAYED WITH THE CROWD, HEADING WEST, AS FAR AS THEY could go. As they walked, more and more people joined the group, traveling mostly on the main roads, but occasionally veering into side streets to get around obstacles. Since The way to Seattle was blocked, they had no choice but to try another direction, and this was their collective choice.

"This is taking too long," James complained.

Luke suffered another bout of coughing before he could say, "It's okay."

"It's not okay. You can barely talk. I can hear you wheezing."

Luke coughed again. This time when he moved his arm from his mouth, there was blood on his shirt. He met James's eyes, saying nothing.

"We have to get inside for a while. Forget staying with the crowd," James said to Jordan.

Jordan saw the blood. He realized James was right. He could let the kids go their own way; they weren't really his problem after all. But thinking about his mom stopped him. She wanted him to save them from that rooftop. She would want him to help them now. He wanted to make her proud, even now, and he would do whatever it took. They were his responsibility now, even if they really weren't. He wasn't going to let anything happen to these kids, and if they needed to get out of the ash, that's what they were going to do.

"Alright," Jordan said. He looked around for the most approachable-looking person. "Excuse me," he called.

A woman turned around.

"Do you know where we're headed?"

"Someone mentioned something about Tacoma. Someone else mentioned Spanaway Lake Park."

"Thank you."

"Those are two different directions," James said under his breath.

The three moved out of the way to stop walking and allow others to pass. A few moments later, they were completely alone, besides the cars parked on the road. Jordan looked around, trying to get his bearings.

"At least we have an idea on where to go. Now, let's head to that street there and start checking houses." He pointed to the front of a gated community a short way down the street.

"It's locked," Luke said from under his shirt.

"That's the point. It should make things a little safer," Jordan said. "Now follow me." He held Chong close to his chest, beneath his sweatshirt, as he led the way.

CHAPTER THIRTY-TWO

Jordan led the way, weaving between the cars, glancing behind him every few minutes to make sure the boys were behind him, and no one else who seemed to be dangerous. After what happened with his mom, he wasn't taking any more chances. He looked down at Chong, through the neck hole in his sweatshirt, who was nuzzled against his stomach for warmth.

"Hey buddy," he whispered.

The dog looked up at him with large brown eyes that looked hopeful.

Jordan didn't have the heart to say anything else.

There were tons of houses to choose from. The problem wasn't the availability of them; it was choosing one that they would be safe in for a while. They needed to be able to stay the night, hopefully until the ash cleared out of the air and they could continue on.

"There," Jordan said, pointing to a ranch-style home at the end of a cul-de-sac.

As they walked toward it, James asked, "What's so special about that one?"

"Nothing. It's just at the end of the road. Let's check it

out. Do either of you have anything you can use as a weapon?"

Luke and James looked at each other. Luke shrugged.

"Like what?" James asked. "I have a few textbooks in my backpack. I can throw them at someone; that has to do some damage."

Jordan smiled. He liked this kid. "That'll have to do," he said.

As they approached the front walk, James walked to the right, around the garage, to peek through to the side of the house and backyard. Luke walked to the left to look through the front windows, while Jordan continued to the front door.

Stepping carefully up the cement path, Jordan looked through the narrow window next to the front door. A sheer curtain hindered his view of the inside, but he could make out the shapes of some of the furniture. He knew if someone was inside, they would be on high alert, possibly dangerous if it was the wrong kind of person.

Whoever lived there might be afraid of intruders and looters. They could be welcoming, eager to help, or not. Worst case, it could be someone who didn't belong, looking for trouble. Just like they'd run into before. Jordan swallowed the lump in his throat. Chong wiggled against his firm grip.

"Hello?" he called.

On the right side of the house, James was on his tippy-toes, looking through the small window on the garage's side door. A car was parked inside. He'd already peeked through the slats on the backyard fence. A manicured lawn was back there, and nothing else. "Nothing over here," he whisper-yelled, not knowing if Jordan heard him or not.

Luke stood in front of the large picture window, leaning over the front hedges, trying to see inside. The curtains were drawn but there were gaps that he thought he could see through if he focused. He heard Jordan's call. There seemed to be movement inside. Was it a cat? He pressed his forehead against the glass, trying to see.

There was a couch, a TV, an open concept with a kitchen island. What was that to the right? He angled his body the other direction, trying to get a better view. The crack between the curtains was minuscule, but Luke had great vision. It was dark inside. Shadows were everywhere. Was that a person standing there?

He felt a cough rising. Luke tried to fight it but there was nothing he could do. He heard Jordan's knock on the front door three times, firm and loud. There it was—movement, again. Luke's eyes grew wide when he finally saw what was inside. He nearly doubled over from his coughing, struggling to catch his breath.

"No!" he croaked.

"There's no one around the side," James said, approaching Jordan and the front door.

Luke tried to run. He could barely breathe, could barely put one foot in front of the other through his lack of oxygen. He waved his arms in a frantic effort to get their attention, but they couldn't see him. He stumbled over himself, trying to get to them before the door opened.

"No!" he cried again between coughs.

Jordan heard. He turned toward Luke, concerned because he was coughing again. He took a step toward him, trading places with James. James tried the door handle. "It's unlocked," he said.

Luke's eyes bulged. His face was drained of all color. He

reached forward. Jordan took another step toward him, patting him on the back. "It's okay, we'll get you inside."

Tears fell from Luke's eyes.

James pushed the door open.

A shotgun blast filled the air.

JAMES'S EARS WERE RINGING. HE STUMBLED BACKWARD, TOO stunned to realize he was still alive, when he shouldn't be. The man in front of him was holding a shotgun pointed into the air, with smoke coming out of the barrel. He was saying something, but James couldn't hear him through the ringing.

He looked down. Was that blood? He took a step backward as the man in front of him lowered the shotgun to the level of his stomach. It finally dawned on him that this man was going to kill him.

James took another step backward and nearly jumped out of his skin when a hand grasped his shoulder. He turned to see Jordan, who was drained of all color. He was saying something, but James still couldn't hear. "What?" he yelled, pointing to his ears. "My ears are ringing."

Jordan pulled him away. They ran as fast as they could, ignoring Luke's coughing, ignoring the blood trickling out from James's ears, ignoring the man still holding the gun. They ran until they were back to the safety of the crowd of people.

CHAPTER THIRTY-THREE

Jordan looked at James, analyzing his face. He forced him to lift his shirt to make sure there weren't any bullet holes. He turned his head from side to side, noting the dried blood that came from his ear canals. "Can you hear yet?" he asked.

"A little," James answered, still yelling.

"How were you not shot?"

"I don't know. He aimed up, I guess."

Jordan felt Chong's shaking. The little dog had to be scared to death. He peeked inside his sweatshirt at the dog, who was cowering against his body for protection. "Hang in there, Chong, buddy. I'm sorry about this," Jordan whispered.

Luke was silent as Jordan looked over James to make sure he wasn't going to drop dead and over Chong to make sure he was still alive too. All he could think about was what could've happened and how he didn't say anything. How he *couldn't.* James and Jordan could've both been dead because he was too choked up.

"What was that guy doing with a shotgun? What kind of person would shoot like that without saying anything?" James asked. He started crying, the shock finally worn off. He hid his face, ashamed to cry in front of the others. Two near-death experiences were a lot for a kid to handle.

Jordan sighed. "Some people are assholes. There's no explanation, no reason. They just are. When they're scared, that's when the worst comes out. That guy back there"—he pointed—"was just some asshole more worried about his eighty-inch TV, than killing someone."

James sniffed, wiping his eyes. "I know."

Jordan looked at Luke, who still hadn't spoken. He wasn't coughing anymore, for the moment, at least. He had his T-shirt pulled up over his nose and mouth to block the ash. "How are you?" he asked Luke.

"Fine," came his muffled reply.

Jordan looked up. "It looks like the ash might be slowing down. It should make things better." He looked around, seeing everything covered, knowing it would still be in the air for weeks, even after this was all over. Even if it wasn't, the smoke would be.

"I'm sorry," Luke said. He couldn't meet either of their eyes.

"Hey," Jordan said, grabbing his shoulders.

The three of them stopped walking.

"You have nothing to be sorry for. You tried. It wasn't your fault. None of this is your fault," Jordan said, looking straight at Luke.

Tears fell from Luke's eyes. He said nothing.

"He's right. It wasn't your fault. There was nothing you could do," James said. "And if you really want to blame your-self, I mean you shouldn't, but if you do, you already saved me once. So, we're even. We're square, Luke. Don't live with even a minute of guilt." He grinned, his most carefree, worry-free smile he could muster, which made Luke cry harder.

Luke gave each of them a quick hug then wiped his eyes. "Let's get outta here." He took off without them, catching up to the crowd in front.

As they walked, people kept joining the crowd until there were so many in their group, it spanned from one sidewalk, across the road, to the sidewalk on the other side. Eventually, the crowd split in two.

"Are we just giving up on finding a safe haven for Luke to get out of this air?" James asked. "I don't like that one guy bullied us into submission."

"I don't like it either," Jordan said. He looked at Luke, who was struggling to breathe without coughing. "How are you holding up?" he asked.

"I'm okay," Luke said. "I don't want to waste any more time." He coughed before continuing. "We're staying with the group. No more taking unnecessary risks."

"Unnecessary risks? Look at you! You can barely speak a sentence without coughing all over the place," James said.

Jordan was torn between the two. He didn't want Luke to drop dead from lack of oxygen intake. His ribs were probably already bruised from all the coughing. He saw him holding his side. But Luke was right too. If he insisted he was okay, they needed to keep moving. Was it really worth chancing another crazy asshole with a gun?

"If he says he's fine, then we're going to keep going. If he gets worse, we'll stop, but we're almost to Pacific Avenue. From there it's a home stretch," Jordan said.

"Home stretch? Have we decided which way to go?" James asked.

"The lady back there gave us two choices. My bet is on Tacoma. Luke said his mom works there anyway, so I say we follow that part of the crowd when it breaks that way." He looked at James. "Now are you ready to stop complaining? It's making him talk and he needs to rest his throat. What we need is some water. Why don't you start looking through some of the empty cars for water bottles?"

James didn't look happy but didn't argue. He ran ahead to look through some cars.

Luke avoided looking Jordan in the eyes. He kept his focus on his feet or straight ahead with the crowd, as Jordan came in and out of his peripheral vision. "How are you?" he whispered.

"Me? I'm not the one who got shot at."

"But you could've been. Easily. You were right there."

Jordan shook his head. "No sense thinking about it. A person could go crazy thinking about all the things that could've happened to them."

Luke was silent for a moment then spoke again. "Alright. I wasn't really talking about that, anyway. I was talking about you know—" He looked away.

"What?"

"Your… your mom. And all that."

Jordan ground his teeth together, taking a moment before speaking. "I'm trying not to think about that either."

"Sorry."

"It's fine."

"I can't help but think about it," Luke admitted. "What if we run into those people again?"

"If we run into them again, we'll just have to be smarter. I won't let anyone hurt you," Jordan said.

"They wanted to *take* us. What do you think they wanted with us?"

Jordan clenched his fists. He didn't know for sure, but had a good idea what people like that planned on doing with kids they kidnapped. "I don't know," he said. "If they really wanted you, they would've taken you, trust me."

"They were too worried about us warning you. They wanted your car—"

"Let's not talk about it, okay?" Jordan ran a hand through his hair. "I'm sorry. I'm just not ready to talk about it."

Luke nodded. "Okay."

Jordan put a hand on Luke's shoulder. "Like I said, I promise I'm not going to let them hurt you. Not anyone. I remember what those fuckers look like, too. You don't have to worry."

Luke nodded again. It wasn't himself he was really worried about. It was Jordan. The look that came over him when he talked about his mom and the people who hurt her, scared him more than anything. More even than the man in the house with the shotgun.

CHAPTER
THIRTY-FOUR

After the emergency broadcast, Gary wasted no time in gathering everyone at The Farm. They all met in the barn, anticipating what he was going to say. What the plan was. The tension in the air was almost palpable. Gary finally walked in with Rick, smiling and everyone seemed to release the breath they were holding.

"So, Big Brother wants everyone to go to the Tacoma Dome for supplies and a safe haven." He looked around, meeting gazes. "If that's where everyone is going to be, you know what that means?"

He waited.

"That's where we're headed," someone said.

"Bingo, my friend. And does anyone know why?"

This was one of the games Gary liked to play. He asked questions, testing how smart his people were, who had the guts to try answering him. He held high praise for intelligent people. Those who questioned him though, were doomed to receive his wrath. If someone answered with something he didn't like, they were doomed too. If they asked the wrong question, they were doomed. If they said nothing, they could also be called out for that.

It was a gamble from all sides. Gary loved to see the fear

in their eyes, along with the immense pleasure they got from his praise. They were like puppy dogs, just waiting to please him.

"We want the free food?" Felicity dared to ask.

Jose looked at her with raised eyebrows.

"Yes!" Gary turned toward her with shining eyes. "Yes, we do."

Pride shone on Felicity's face. Everyone else looked surprised.

"We want the food, folks, more specifically the prepackaged meals. And the clothes, the batteries, the water bottles, anything we can get our hands on quickly and easily. But there's a bigger aim here."

"Why the hell would we want all that?" someone whispered.

Gary heard but couldn't tell who said it. He let it pass.

"What do we do here, at The Farm?" he asked.

No one was willing to say it out loud.

"We sell people, folks. In case anyone forgot, our valuable commodity needs to stay *alive* while in our possession. How do you keep a person alive?"

"Food!" someone yelled.

"Congratulations, my friend. You're the winner today!" Gary yelled back. "Food and water are what keeps people alive and we're about to get an ass ton of it for free. We can expand our operations and it's going to last for a long time. But that's just the gravy on top. Any guesses what our primary target is? Or should I say primary targets?"

Murmurs went around. The group was finally starting to catch on to Gary's train of thought. More confident in his mood and what kind of answer he was looking for, they were willing to speak up.

"There's going to be a lot of people looking for supplies. A ton of them. They're going to be so focused on getting food that they're not going to be worried about much else," someone said.

"So worried," added another, "that probably not many will be paying attention to their kids."

Gary grinned. They were getting the exact picture he wanted them to see. "That's where our job comes in. We're going to make sure they're too distracted to notice a thing."

"Why don't we just loot some stores?"

Everyone held their breath at the question, afraid it would send Gary reeling. He had a short fuse. All it took was one wrong question or comment to do the job.

Gary surprised them all by remaining calm. "Now, let's think about that for a minute," he said. "Yes, we could loot some stores. That would be easy enough, maybe less risky, maybe not." He waited to see if anyone would throw in another comment.

When no one did, he sighed. "Goods are not our business, people. It all comes back to the business. Sure, we could've gotten some expensive stuff—still probably can. We can even pull up to a grocery store and stock the whole damn Isuzu. There's a point we make by doing what we have planned. There's a *statement* we make. Please tell me someone understands."

"I get it, boss!" someone cried.

"Makes sense to me!"

"I'm with you, Gary!"

Gary smiled, but his heart wasn't in it all the way. He hated having to spell everything out, was somewhat disappointed. He met Rick's eyes then turned back to his people. "If we are powerful enough to steal food from Big Brother, then that makes us pretty goddamn powerful, right?"

"Absolutely!"

"Yes!"

"Hell yeah!"

"Good. That's the message we're sending. Think big picture here. Forget about what I said about our business. Think about our image. We are *powerful.* We will *not* be fucked with. We hold the food; therefore, we hold the power. This volcano bullshit won't last forever, but we don't know how long it *will* last. We don't know how long we're going to be cut off from the rest of the world. When the food is out, people will come to us for protection. That will give us even *more* power."

Everyone in the barn shared looks with each other. As what Gary was saying grew on them, they started to like more and more what they were hearing. Normally their line of business was relatively quiet. They stayed in the shadows, so to speak. But he was going to let them shine a little light.

They would be seen as *powerful.* It was something most of them hadn't thought of before. Cheers erupted in support of the plan.

"Alright folks, we have work to do," Gary said, reveling in the approval of his people. "We have less than twelve hours to be in place. When that chopper drops the supplies, we're gonna make sure we're already in place."

"Yeah!" someone shouted.

"We're gonna get everything we want and then some. There's room for plenty of women, too. Grab the easy ones, boys. I'm looking at you, Rick."

Rick nodded. He got the message.

"Don't waste your time on the ones who are gonna put up a fight," Gary continued. "We've been there already, and it's not worth it. There are so many opportunities in a situation like this, so let's make the most of it. Remember to bring whatever you catch straight back here to The Farm. No detours. Big Brother is gonna put up a fight, but I've got a nice little plan for that."

The others clapped when Gary finished, eager to get on

the road and get their job done. It wasn't every day that a natural disaster occurred. Each secretly wondered how many they'd be able to grab. There was an especially high demand for kids right now, and everyone knew Gary gave bonuses to anyone who caught one. It was going to be easy pickin's.

"Excited to do this?" Felicity asked Jose.

"Yeah. This is my biggest gig yet," he said.

"Mine too." She smiled. "How were you able to text? I still don't have any signal."

"What are you talking about? I wasn't texting anyone."

"I saw your message app open. When Gary was talking." She came closer to whisper in his ear. "I know you were trying to be sly about it."

Jose blushed. "I was *trying* to text, but it didn't go through. Just like you, no signal."

"I thought Gary didn't like anyone on their phones here?" she whispered again. "What's with the phone drop-off thing when we first get to the farm?"

"Yeah. Don't tell anyone, okay? Gary is really private. Can you blame him with all that goes on around here?"

Her eyes lit up. "You wanna tell me about it?"

He grimaced. "Girl, you ask too many questions. You need to cut that shit out."

Felicity pulled him to her before kissing him.

RICK STOOD NEXT TO KEVIN AS THE OTHERS SPLIT INTO TWO teams and loaded into the vehicles. "You're not gonna worry about being cramped, are you Kev? When it comes to loading that rig up with as many kiddies as you can get?" Rick asked, arching his eyebrows.

"Nah," Kevin said. His fists were clenched at his side. He was angry but he knew to keep his mouth shut. Especially after what Gary just did to Felicity.

"Good. I'd hate to have to ask Gary for some reasonable accommodations." Rick smiled. They both understood what it meant. "Listen, I have a special job for you. And keep it on the down low, if you know what I mean."

Kevin's eyes lit up. "About the job?"

"Yeah. About Felicity, specifically."

CHAPTER
THIRTY-FIVE

Tim didn't have to look very hard to find the people in charge at base camp. Two tables were set up in the middle of the room, near racks of supplies that were being handed out to people. He scowled when he saw who was one of the people sitting next to three men in military uniforms.

"If it isn't my favorite boss. How you doing, Joe?" Tim asked, approaching the first table.

Joe looked embarrassed but not surprised to see him. "I tried to call. The cell towers and all the other goddamn phone lines are down."

"You fired me, Joe."

"You jumped the fucking gun. I warned you there was more at play—"

"More at play? People's lives were at stake. Are at stake. Look at this madness." Tim waved an arm around at the room packed full of people who were covered in ash, displaced from their homes, scared and hungry, with no place to go. "This could have turned out much differently."

Joe shook his head. "I know. I'm sorry, Tim. You have to believe me. I'll make this right. I'll give a public apology myself. I'll put you up for a raise. I'll—"

"It's not about me. We need to help these people. Not just these people, but the ones who haven't made it here. What's being done for them? People are going to need food and supplies. Hell, they can't even survive without toilet paper. How are they going to make it without groceries?"

"The National Guard is going to airlift in supplies. We can't get out, but there are still ways to get supplies in to us."

Tim looked skeptical. "They can get in through this kind of air? Ash is still falling. You can barely see anything through the smoke."

Joe scoffed. "They can get through anything."

Tim wasn't sure if Joe knew what he was talking about. He took the information with a grain of salt, ready to speak with the men in uniform an arm's reach away. One of them would be able to verify the validity of what Joe was saying. "Excuse me," he said, addressing the men.

They looked at him with raised eyebrows. "I'm with the US Geological Survey. My boss here is telling me about the helicopter drop that's planned."

"Yes, sir. It's scheduled to drop soon."

"And how is everyone supposed to get these supplies?"

"We sent out a broadcast on the radio. Phone lines and TV are still down. There's nothing else we can do. Word of mouth is crucial, so please tell anyone you come across."

"There's nothing else you can do? You're the US Government, there's got to be loads you can do. What about the JBLM base? Where are all the military?"

The soldier scowled at Tim. "The military has been deployed to help look for survivors and assist police with looting. There are a million tasks and only so many to complete them. In case you didn't know, we're cut off from the rest of the country. It's like we're back in the fifties."

"That can't possibly—"

"I don't care what you believe or think, *sir*. These are the facts. Now look, I don't have time to sit here and argue. I've got a list of things a mile long that need to be taken care of. If you want to help, tell as many people as you can that supplies will be handed out soon. Go see the volunteer table over there and they'll get you set up with something to do." He pointed to a small table across the way, with people holding clipboards. Without waiting for an answer from Tim, the man in uniform walked away with the other men he'd been speaking to.

"Do you think it will be enough?" Tim asked Joe.

"It'll have to be," Joe said. "Like he said, the broadcast already went out. I'm sure they'll repeat it all day long. People have been flowing in through those doors. They know to come here."

Tim clenched his fists. He didn't like how things were being run and he didn't like that he didn't have a better idea or any power to change things. "I met a woman who's trying to find her son. Is there anything that can be done to help people find loved ones?"

"Not with communications still down. All we have is the check-in man in the tent out front."

"Does anyone get past him?"

"Nope. Check-in required for all who enter."

Tim pressed his lips, thinking. "Thanks, Joe."

He walked back to where he left Teresa. He didn't have an idea of the time, but thought they'd been there longer than she had wanted. By the time they checked in, looked for Luke, and then had his little chat with Joe, Tim thought it had to be past midday by now. Probably close to two, or three, even.

He reached the spot where they'd been standing together, where he thought she'd be waiting, but Teresa wasn't there. Tim's eyes narrowed in confusion. "Maybe she's looking for Luke again," he said to himself.

Tim walked through the building again, looking for Teresa and calling out for her. When he made it back to his original spot again, it hit him. "She left without me."

Anger at being tricked, and worry for her safety, over-whelmed him. Tim thought about running out to chase after her, but wasn't sure about the head start she had. What if he was wrong and she really was still here somewhere, and he just didn't see her? What if she was just in the bathroom?

Tim's mind reeled with the choice he had to make. He was determined to keep his promise to her one way or another. At the same time, there was a building full of other people he could try helping. He could get supplies, go back toward Rainier, help anyone out there who was trapped or lost.

"There have to be hundreds back in Elbe, still," he said. The more he thought about it, the surer he was. He had to get back out there. There was no sense in him staying inside just to wait on a woman who didn't want his help.

CHAPTER THIRTY-SIX

"Thanks for everything, Tim," Teresa whispered to herself, heading for the doors. He was still over there talking to some soldiers, and she was taking her chance to leave without him.

When those men tried to grab her from her car, she'd been afraid. Afraid that if something happened to her, she'd never see Luke again. Afraid they would keep her from him. Teresa was still terrified to go out there alone but wasn't going to let fear stop her anymore. "Please don't let this be a mistake," she muttered as she walked out of the building and back into the check-in tent.

Teresa was the only one leaving. Everyone else was in line to get in. "Excuse me," she called to the man at the check-in.

He was distracted, flustered, busy doing five things at once. "Just a moment, please," he called back without looking.

"I'm leaving and I wanted to leave a contact number if my son checks in. For when the phones are back up."

He ignored her, continued with his business.

She waited.

Still, he said nothing. He forgot about her already.

Teresa put herself in front of him. "I'm leaving. I need to leave my contact info in case my son checks in."

He finally looked at her, eyes full of irritation. "Are you checked in already?"

"Yes."

"Then we have your info."

"But I want to make sure—"

"Do you see this line of people?" he snapped, pointing at the line extending out of the tent, winding through the parking lot.

Teresa looked.

He glared at her.

She got the point. He was too busy to help her and if she wanted his time, she was going to have to wait. She sighed. She wasn't trying to cut; she was just hoping he'd answer a simple question. But she understood. Teresa walked away.

"Teresa?"

She spun around.

"Nate!"

He ran to her, hugged her.

"I have to leave," she said. "My son isn't here."

"Where's Tim?"

"I'm going alone."

His eyebrows furrowed, not understanding. "Take me with you."

"No, honey. You're safer here. And aren't you helping with the dogs? I'm sure they really appreciate you."

Nate scoffed. "Yeah right. All I'm doing is picking up poop. They don't even let me feed them. No one is even paying attention to me. I don't feel any safer here than being with you and Tim. And besides"—he leaned close to her ear —"they're starting to complain." Nate nodded his head toward the line of people.

Teresa looked at them more closely. She could see some

of them grumbling among themselves. "I'm sure they're just tired of waiting in line. That's normal."

"I think it's more than that. Please, Teresa, let me go with you."

She didn't have the heart to walk away from him. "Okay," she said. "Let's get out of here."

Nate started to head back toward the dogs. "I'll just grab—"

"No, leave him here. He's safer here."

Nate looked at her with pleading eyes, but knew she was right. There were kennels and even though everyone was busy, the dogs were still in a safe place, being watched after. It was better than roaming the streets with the humans, where only God knew what could happen. He finally nodded in agreement. "Okay, I'll just say goodbye to him."

"We're experiencing some turbulence, sir," the helicopter pilot said. "Zero visibility. She's not liking this wind."

"You don't need to see, soldier. Pay attention to your instruments," came a firm reply through the radio.

"Yes, sir."

Ash and smoke covered every inch of his view, swirling from the natural wind and that caused by the chopper's propellers. His grip held firm when a gust hit. "Shit!" he cried.

"Almost there," the copilot said through gritted teeth.

Warning lights started going off.

"This isn't good. Hang on!"

It felt weird to be walking through a city she normally only drove through. Teresa looked at the horizon. "A couple of hours before dark probably," she said, walking with high hopes as fast as she could. It got dark early in November; the season was working against them.

Her best bet at this point was to head home. She'd been thinking about nothing but where Luke would go, and she was gambling it all on home. Puyallup was flooded, but not the whole city, and if their house was caught in the worst of it then she'd try the school next. He could've stayed there after all. She just hoped he wasn't hurt.

Tim was kind to help her. He was more than kind—he saved her life. He didn't owe her a thing, no matter what promise he made, and she was tired of waiting. Tim had his own responsibilities, things he needed to take care of. She didn't want to slow him down any more than she wanted to be slowed down.

Teresa knew she had to get out of there and keep looking for Luke. She couldn't take the chance that something had happened to him, and he was out there needing her. After what Naomi said about the chaos at the school, Teresa's heart hurt for her boy more now than ever.

After twenty minutes of walking, Teresa was starting to second-guess her decision. She was torn between the very real possibility that her son was at home waiting for her, and had been all this time, and between the possibility that he was now checked in at base camp, *waiting* for her there. *What if he was there, and I walked right past him? she thought.*

She pulled out her phone. "Still no signal."

"How long until you get one, do you think?" Nate asked.

"I'm not sure. It could be a while. Probably until we're not cut off anymore, I imagine."

They kept walking. "I'll find him, eventually. He's safe," she said, mostly to herself. She repeated the words over and over as a reminder that this would all be over sooner or later. The majority of the Puget Sound wasn't going to be cut off from the rest of the world forever. Communications would come back up any time. The dust would settle, and supplies would get through.

Nate didn't know what to say, so he didn't say anything. He let Teresa say what she needed to say.

"If people in the south live through hurricanes every year, we can make it through this," she told herself. She didn't want to think about the number of people who died from them every year or all the damage that went along with them, only that people did *survive*.

They heard a helicopter in the distance. Teresa looked up, shielding her eyes from the setting sun, from the ash that was still falling, and the smoke that was covering everything.

"Something isn't right," she said.

"Sir, the pilot isn't responding."

"What do you mean, he's not responding? They're supposed to be landing in"—he checked his watch,—"any minute!"

"Comms were cut off just moments ago. The pilot was complaining about the wind."

"The wind. The goddamned wind!" He threw the papers off his desk in a fit of rage. "I need to know what's happening with that helicopter."

"Yes, sir."

Outside, Captain Blake was trying to somehow keep from crashing on top of the evacuees at base camp. The helicopter was coming down fast, and he had little control. A rooftop wasn't going to happen. This baby was going on the ground.

Jose pointed up. "There it is."

Felicity squinted. "It looks out of control."

They watched as the helicopter swayed back and forth in the sky. It dipped before pulling up hard and then falling again.

Jose turned to Rick, who was smiling.

"It looks like there's going to be a slight change of plans," Rick said.

A helicopter was barely visible overhead, back in the direction of the Tacoma Dome. It looked low. Teresa knew nothing about helicopters or what height they were supposed to travel, but this one looked like it was dipping and swerving.

"How can he even see?" Nate asked.

It was coming closer. And lower. It dawned on Teresa what was about to happen. "Oh my God, is it going to crash?"

They stopped walking to watch the helicopter go down. Seconds later, they heard the crash. "Oh my God!" Teresa covered her mouth with a hand, unable to believe what she just saw and heard.

Then she thought about all the people who were in the building and outside, waiting to get in. She thought about Tim, still there and probably looking for her. She wondered if he even realized she was gone yet. Then she wondered where the helicopter went down.

"Tim!" Nate cried.

"We have to go back," Teresa whispered. She clenched her fists, angry at the situation, angry at herself *again* for not acting sooner. "We have to see where it landed."

They turned back toward the Tacoma Dome. She had to see if Tim was hurt and since she was only about a mile out, she thought they could run most of the way. Teresa just had to see for herself and then if there was nothing she could do, she would turn right back around and continue toward home.

CHAPTER
THIRTY-SEVEN

The line to get checked in at base camp was steadily growing longer. At this point, some had been waiting for what felt like hours. It was slow going with only a small portion of personnel available to help and only a handful of volunteers.

With the long wait came frustration, short tempers, and high tension. The supply drop was today. It was why everyone came out of the woodwork to wait. After over twenty-four hours of being cut off from the rest of the state and the rest of the world, there wasn't a single person around not eager to get their share of provisions, and everyone was worried there wouldn't be enough left for them.

"What's taking so long?" someone asked from the back of the line. They were loud enough for those in the front to hear. Some shifted around, looking back to see who the complainer was.

Some in the middle started to mumble their agreement. "Yeah, this is ridiculous," came another remark.

"Must have to sign our lives away before they let us in."

"My family just wants to eat. Why won't they just give us food?"

The complaints steadily grew until people were talking

among themselves, unease and distrust growing from a hum to something much louder. Those who were toward the back were loudest, but some in the middle and front were just as tired of waiting.

"We're moving as fast as we can. We appreciate everyone's patience," the man up front said. He looked nervous. He was well aware of how quickly things could go south if a crowd of people decided they didn't want to listen to the rules. He started to speak faster, urging people through without answering questions. He was trying to do his job, but he didn't want this to get ugly.

"Why are we even waiting here?" someone asked a few minutes later. "We should just go through. Why do they need us to check in?"

Murmured agreement came.

"Why do you need our names? What does it matter?"

"I'm going in. Who's with me?" A man started to walk forward, around those who were already in line. Another followed, and then another. When those who had been waiting before them saw what was happening, they weren't about to let them get through before they did. Not after all their waiting.

People started rushing forward, angry at those who were now refusing to wait, angry that they had to wait at all. They were hungry, frightened, and tired of feeling displaced. "Wait!" the man up front cried. "Please, everyone, just wait a minute and calm down."

"We're tired of waiting!" a woman yelled back.

"I'm going to need some help over here!" he yelled.

A few other official-looking people came over to try diffusing the situation, but their presence seemed to intensify the anger. What was once a quiet line was now distorted and morphed into a mob of furious faces, all pushing their way forward.

"I have children here. Please don't push them!" a woman cried, trying to get her kids out of the way. There were others who wanted no part of what was happening. They just wanted food for themselves or their families. They would wait if that was what was needed. They didn't want to fight anyone.

Jordan watched the woman try to shield her child from a man pushing his way forward. He saw an old woman with fear in her eyes and it reminded him of his mom. He clenched his fists at the absurdity of the scene. Innocent people could get hurt very easily if something wasn't done.

James and Luke saw it too. "Hey, I don't mind waiting," James called out, trying to help defuse the situation.

"Yeah, it's nice to be covered under these tents, out of the ash," Luke added as loud as he could.

"You're fucking kids, that's why you don't mind!" someone called back.

"Exactly," Jordan roared in the direction the yell came from. "There are kids here, motherfuckers. Calm the hell down."

A few took heed, realized what was happening and seemed to second-guess their actions. But it wasn't enough to make a difference. There were too many angry individuals.

Moments passed in a rush. The crowd's fuse was lit and there was no stopping it. The instigators were now at the front, pushing people through into the camp. Once through, they ran. "Where's the supplies?" one asked.

"They're probably inside."

"I'll check that tent."

"Please, everyone. The supply shipment hasn't arrived yet."

Some started to slow at that announcement. If the shipment wasn't there yet, what were they in a rush for?

"It doesn't matter. There's still food here, somewhere," someone called.

As the mob rushed forward, through those who were already in base camp, pandemonium broke out. Those who were already there waiting, saw the mob rushing forward and panicked. Some of the mob attacked people who were eating, stealing the food from their hands.

Some started going through belongings. Others tried to fight them off. Fists flew, along with blood. A handful of people had weapons—knives, and even guns. A shot rang out, followed by screaming. There were two policemen in the building, and other than them and a handful of soldiers, no other form of authority to stop the chaos.

A large portion of the mob was headed for the stockpile of water, blankets, and other supplies in the middle of the dome. Another part of the group seemed to be attacking anyone they could. It didn't matter what they had to steal, they just wanted to beat innocent people for the hell of it.

Jordan, Luke, and James tried to help who they could but there was little they could do in the middle of a moving throng. They were pushed forward along with everyone else.

As the crowd formed into a frenzied mob, an explosion outside rocked the building. Everyone stopped and for a split second, there was calm. "What was that?" someone asked.

Murmurs and speculation spread like wildfire until someone yelled, "The helicopter!"

"That way!" Rick called, waving his group forward. They led the way toward the crash.

CHAPTER THIRTY-EIGHT

"Run!" Rick yelled, sprinting toward the crash. He was caught up in the moment, ready for any possibility. They'd done a good job at riling up the crowd. People who were already angry and afraid like that were easy to manipulate. They were like sheep, just waiting to be led the right way.

Now came the harder part. "Jose, left. Kev, you go right," Rick instructed.

The chopper had crashed halfway into the parking lot, halfway on the street. There wasn't much damage to anything else but the helicopter. It lay on its side, the nose was scraped and crushed in, along with the propellers that hit the pavement.

The pilots were visible. They were slumped forward in their seats, probably passed out. "Make it quick. There's no fire now but you know how these things go," Rick said.

"Yeah, watch it blow up in our faces." Felicity laughed.

The others ignored her, moving forward. It looked like things had fallen out in the crash. There was something all over the pavement around the helicopter. Jose and his group came up around the left side to find water bottles thrown everywhere.

"Nothing but water bottles over here," he called out.

"Same," Kevin said from the right side.

They had seconds before company joined them.

Jordan tried to keep Luke and James away from the swarm headed toward the doors. People were plowing each other over, trying to get to that helicopter. "We need to get as far away from them as we can," he yelled. With everyone screaming and crying out, it was almost too loud to be heard.

The boys clung to him as he led the way against the crowd, toward the back of the building. People pushed past. "Get out of the fucking way!" one yelled.

"Move it, asshole!" another cried.

Luke let go of Jordan to cover his ears with both hands. He ducked his head down into his chest, trying to stay as small as possible. As unnoticeable as possible. Someone bumped into him. Luke staggered backward, then pushed his way forward again. When he looked up, Jordan and James were gone.

"Jordan?" he called. "James?" It was too loud for them to hear.

Jordan and James finally reached an area where there were no people, and realized that Luke was not with them. They looked toward the crowd where everyone seemed to be fighting each other to get through the doors. They looked at each other and then walked back into the frenzy.

"Let's stick together," Jordan said. "We can't risk getting split up again."

"They should all be out the doors soon, shouldn't they?"

"You would think, but who knows what some idiot is going to try pulling? Just stick by me."

They both called for Luke, and although the crowd was slimming, they still couldn't find him. "Do you think he went outside?" James asked.

"He could've gotten turned around."

FROM THE MIDDLE OF THE BUILDING, TIM WATCHED THE moment the crash registered on people's faces. It was food they were worried about, and from that second, the majority of people who were panicked and terrified turned into something wild.

He clearly saw those who were only trying to get away from the crazy ones, and the crazy ones who would do anything to get to the much-needed supplies. There were people outside yelling, trying to get in and then it seemed once they were in, something shifted in the air. The crash came and now they were all trying to get back out.

Tim saw a boy who was bent over, holding his ears. He looked alone and like he was about to be trampled. "Hey, watch out for that kid," he called, trying to get to him. No one paid any attention.

Tim watched the boy get pushed forward and shoved to the side. He was crying with his eyes closed. Tim didn't know what he was thinking but knew if someone didn't help him, there was no doubt he'd be hurt.

When he finally reached the kid, he guided him out of the way of most of the crowd. "It's okay," he said. "I'm not going to hurt you."

The boy was still crying, refusing to look at him.

"My name is Tim. What's yours?"

Still no answer, but Tim was glad to see that the crying had stopped. He was sniffling now, wiping his nose and eyes. Finally, the boy looked at Tim and Tim almost fell down from shock at recognizing him from his photo.

"I'm Luke," the boy said.

Tim couldn't believe it. "Luke, is your mom's name Teresa?"

Luke began to cry again. "Yes." He sniffed. "Do you know her?"

Tim laughed. He threw his arms up like this was the best news he'd heard all year. "Yep, I know her alright. I've been helping her try to find you."

Luke's eyes grew wide. "Is she here?"

"No. At least, I don't think so."

"What does that mean?"

"We were supposed to meet back up, but she wasn't there. I looked everywhere for her and I'm pretty sure she left me here to go looking for you again. Her worry for you was eating her alive."

Luke looked stricken.

"I'm not saying it's your fault. Don't think that for a minute," Tim said.

Luke nodded.

"We better get out of here. God, I'm glad I hung around for a minute. We can try to catch up with your mom now. I'm not sure which way she was headed though, she never said. Do you have any ideas? Maybe your home?"

"I'm with some others. I need to find them first." Luke started to look around and spotted Jordan headed his way. "Speak of the devil."

CHAPTER
THIRTY-NINE

James rushed forward and grabbed Luke in a bear hug. "We were so worried about you."

"I got a little turned around," Luke said, blushing.

"Are you okay?" Jordan asked. "I'm sorry I lost you."

"No—yes, I'm fine. You didn't lose me, I let go."

Jordan looked Luke over then turned toward Tim. "Who are you?"

"He helped me," Luke said. "He knows my mom."

Jordan's eyes widened.

"I'm Tim. Nice to meet you." Tim stuck out his hand to shake.

"Jordan." Jordan shook. "This is James," he said, patting James on the shoulder.

"Nice to meet you, James." Tim looked back at Jordan. "I was just telling Luke that his mom isn't here. She left to go look for him. It hasn't been very long. We might be able to catch up with her."

"We need to hurry!" Luke cried.

"Hang on, hang on." Jordan scrutinized Tim. "How do we know this isn't a trap? We've been through a lot to get here.

I'm not exactly willing to trust strangers again anytime soon."

Tim held up his hands in mock surrender. "I understand, and it's wise of you to question everything. I'm not sure how to put your mind at ease, other than to give you my word. Teresa and I have been through a lot today ourselves. I promised her I'd help her find Luke and I'm not going to rest until I do."

Luke looked between the two men. He studied Tim's face. "I trust you," he said.

Tim smiled. "Thank you, Luke."

Jordan must've seen whatever Luke saw. "Alright then," he said.

THE SOUND OF DOGS BARKING WAS THE FIRST THING THEY heard when they stepped back through the doors. They saw that all the dogs were still in the kennels under the tents that were now abandoned. It looked like the check-in man was trying to calm them down.

"I don't see Nate," Tim said.

"Who's Nate?" Luke asked.

"A boy I was with. He was supposed to be with the dogs. I wonder if he went with your mom."

"Do you want to look for him?"

Tim walked to the dogs in the kennels and searched until he found the one he was looking for. "Hey, buddy, there you are." He stuck his hand through the bars to rub the top of the dog's head. "I don't think he would go anywhere without this dog," Tim said. "I think he's here somewhere."

They started to walk.

Luke looked toward the helicopter that was swarmed with people. "What happens if there's no more food?" he asked. "Maybe we should try to get some too."

"We'll find food eventually. We should be more worried about getting away from that crowd," Jordan said.

"But—"

"He's right," Tim said. "Trust me, Luke. A mob like that is not something you want to mess with."

Luke couldn't stop staring. They were walking away, and he was falling behind again. He just couldn't stop looking at the things people were doing to each other.

He gasped. "Jordan."

Jordan sighed. He turned back toward Luke, seeing the look on his face—like he'd seen a ghost. "What is it?"

All the color drained from Luke's face. He couldn't look away. Couldn't even blink. His voice caught. Jordan shook him. "What the hell is it, Luke?"

"It's… It's them. The one's from the rooftop."

They all looked to where Luke was pointing. Tim didn't know who they were seeing but he could tell it wasn't good. "Who are we seeing here, guys?" he asked.

THEY WERE ALL SILENT, STARING. JORDAN COULDN'T BELIEVE his eyes. It was them alright. Them. Him. His fists clenched. Everything else melted away from existence as he stared at the man who killed his mother.

The man was holding a gun, waving it around. It looked like he was giving orders, yelling something. Others were listening to him. The others who were with him on the rooftop.

Chong was in his hoodie pocket, poking his head out. He seemed to be staring at them too. He was shaking and emitting a low growl.

"Someone has to make them pay," Jordan said, talking to himself. He started walking toward the helicopter.

"Whoa, whoa," Tim said. "Can someone please talk to me here? I thought we were trying to get away from this. We're going to find Teresa, right?"

"It's the ones who killed his mom," James said.

"They what?"

Three lifted trucks came flying in from the road with a large Isuzu box truck behind them. In the beds of the pickups were people holding guns.

"Get down," Tim yelled.

They all dropped except for Jordan.

"Jordan!" James called.

The people in the trucks flew past them, headed straight for the helicopter. They fired their guns, shooting anyone who was within their sights. Gunfire rained down on the crowd. People began shooting at each other, and at the military, who was until now, present but uninvolved.

Now that there were shots fired, they stood their ground. The military was firing back. People were running in all directions, flooding the parking lot and street, no longer swarming the helicopter.

"We need to all get the hell out of here," Tim said.

Jordan was still out of it, now walking toward the helicopter. He didn't have a plan. All he knew was that he had to do something. Had to bring down his mom's murderer. He ground his teeth together until his jaw ached, never losing sight of the man who ended her life just to steal her car.

Chong wiggled in his pocket. Jordan finally looked down at him. He turned back to James. "Take Chong."

TIM WATCHED JORDAN HAND HIS LITTLE DOG OVER TO JAMES, and then continue toward the helicopter. He could only imagine the man's pain at seeing his mother's murderer but how could he let him walk to what would probably be his death? "Jordan, stop," he called.

"I have to do something."

"We need to at least talk about this."

"There's no time."

Luke went to follow. "He's right. We have to do something."

Tim couldn't believe what he was seeing. "What about your mom?" he called.

"She would understand."

"This isn't your fight!" Tim demanded.

They kept walking. Tim stood next to James, watching them. James turned to him, still holding Chong. "What are we going to do?"

Looking at Chong made Tim think of Nate and the dog they'd found. *What happened to Nate?* he wondered, still not catching sight of him. His mind started to spin as the added concern put more pressure on his shoulders.

"We don't have long before Jordan and Luke get themselves into trouble." Tim put his hands on James's shoulders. "Will you stay here with the dog? I need to help them, and I need at least one damn person around here to be safe."

James nodded, almost looking relieved. "I'll watch Chong. We'll stay out of it."

Tim blew out a breath. "Thank you. I mean it." He took off running.

CHAPTER FORTY

Teresa and Nate were both out of breath, but neither slowed down or stopped running. "Almost there," Teresa panted, holding a stitch in her side. When she had a view of the parking lot, her step faltered.

"What is it?" Nate asked.

"The helicopter crashed into the parking lot. Look." They picked up speed, watching the chaos play out around the wreckage. The military was there, but not very many of them. Guns were being fired. People were running all over the place.

"Do you think Tim is there still?" Nate asked.

They finally slowed down the road several hundred feet before the entrance to the parking lot. As soon as they were close enough to see the check-in tent, Teresa saw Tim. "There he is," she said.

"Where?"

"Over there. He's talking to a kid who's holding a little chihuahua." She pointed in his direction.

"He's running away," Nate said.

"Tim!" Teresa called but he was too far already. He didn't hear, but the kid he was with did. He turned toward Teresa and Nate with eyes like saucers.

"Hey," she said. She ran the rest of the way to him. "Where is Tim going?"

"He's running after Jordan and Luke."

"Luke?" She took a step toward him. "What does Luke look like? How old?"

The kid gulped. "Are you Teresa?"

That was all it took. She knew it was *her* Luke and something was wrong. "Nate, stay here," she said, then took off running after Tim.

EVERYTHING WAS GOING ACCORDING TO PLAN. THEY HAD THE supplies. Team two showed up with the guns and the trucks. They were holding Big Brother off easily. "Those pansies are too worried about hitting civilians," Rick called out to his team. "Stay close to them, and we're home free."

They loaded all the captives first, and then the rest of the supplies into the trucks, ducking as the occasional shot fired overhead. The military was fighting back, but barely. There were only a handful of soldiers that hadn't been deployed when Rainier first erupted, and now they were paying the price for their lack of numbers. Until the National Guard decided to show up, at least.

Rick and his people weren't going to be able to fit everything they wanted, but they were packed to the gills with people. "Rick!" Kevin called.

"What?"

"Look!" Kevin pointed to the two figures who were coming toward them instead of running away.

Rick's jaw dropped, recognizing them immediately.

"YOU KILLED MY MOM!" JORDAN SCREAMED. HE CHARGED toward Rick, who was too stunned to point his gun. Jordan slammed into him, knocking the pistol from his hand. They fell to the blacktop in a heap, fists flying.

"What the fuck is happening?" someone screamed.

"It's the guy who got us off the rooftop," Kevin said.

"Oh, shit!"

"Shoot him!" Felicity yelled.

"No! You might hit Rick," Jose said.

Luke stood back out of the way, watching like the rest. He saw the gun that nobody else seemed to notice and played with the idea of grabbing it. He took a step forward, then waited to see if someone would say something.

"She was just an old woman, you sick fuck!" Jordan screamed. They rolled in front of Luke, forcing him to retreat. Jordan saw the gun now. When he reached for it, Rick punched him in the gut. Tears sprang to Jordan's eyes as he gasped for air.

"She could've stepped out of the car. It's not my fault," Rick said.

"You're deluded!" Jordan choked.

They continued beating each other into a bloody mess. Rick had to be nearly twice Jordan's size, but it didn't seem to have much hold against Jordan's heartache and need for justice.

They rolled closer to the gun. Rick inched his body forward. Jordan reached up to gouge his eyes. Rick cried out in fury, swinging at full force. While he wiped the blood from his vision, Jordan got the gun.

He didn't wait a heartbeat. He pulled the trigger, blowing Rick's brains all over the blacktop.

"Fuck!" Felicity, Kevin, and all the others collectively yelled.

Jordan pointed the gun toward them before noticing how close Luke was.

Kevin pulled Luke in next to his chest and held his gun to the back of his neck. "I'd think a little harder this time, if I was you," he said.

"Let him go. He's got nothing to do with this," Jordan said.

"Put the gun down, friend. Your beef with Rick is over."

Jordan took a step back and lowered the gun.

"Drop it."

Jordan dropped it.

Kevin smiled as he moved the gun from Luke to Jordan. Jordan knew he was about to see his mom again. He saw Kevin's finger tighten on the trigger. Kevin swung the gun away, aiming right at Felicity.

Her eyes nearly bulged out of her head. "Kev—"

He pulled the trigger. Everyone's ears were ringing; they were all shocked to their core, including Jordan.

"Just a little problem I had to take care of. Now, where were we?" Kevin said. He swung the gun back toward Jordan. Both their heads jerked again when a voice yelled, "Stop!"

The trigger squeezed, missing its target. Jordan ducked while Tim ran forward. Someone else shot at them, missing again. Luke tried to pull himself free, but Kevin held him tighter than ever. "You're not going anywhere," he growled.

"Tim!" Luke yelled.

They were pulling him away, piling back into the trucks. He fought harder but it didn't matter. He was no match for the strength of a grown man who was used to holding back struggling kids.

"LUKE!" TERESA WAILED, HARDLY ABLE TO BREATHE.

"Mom!" Luke cried. "Mom, don't let them take me!" Luke swung his arms wildly, trying to hit anyone he could. He came into contact with someone, and they hit him back twice as hard.

Luke's head flung back. His vision darkened.

Teresa ran forward, trying to push her way through. She ignored the gunshots, ignored someone trying to pull her back, ignored everything. Luke was here. He was alive. And now he was being taken from her. She hadn't even had a chance to hold him. It was too late.

"LUKE!" TIM RAN FORWARD, ONLY STOPPING WHEN SOMEONE shot. He watched them pull Luke into one of the trucks. "Jordan, we have to do something!"

Tim wasn't normally one to panic. He didn't even panic when no one would listen to him about Rainier. But now he was panicking. He found Teresa's son, only to get him abducted by a bunch of murderers. How was he ever going to get him back? And in one piece?

"No!" Tim screamed at the top of his lungs when the truck carrying Luke started to drive away. He ran past Teresa, chasing after it. He followed for as long as he could. Tim didn't make it far before he fell to his knees screaming, as the driver of the truck floored it.

CHAPTER FORTY-ONE

Jordan sat silent, holding Teresa back. He was more torn than he could've ever imagined being. On one hand, he had his revenge. Sweet, sweet revenge. Jordan never dreamed it would be his so *soon*.

On the other hand, he'd been rash, irresponsible, stupid. He'd just killed a man. Jordan didn't want to even start to think how his parents would view him now. And how could he have let Luke follow him into the lion's den like that? Jordan had hardly even paid attention to his presence. Luke could've easily been shot. What was Luke even thinking following him like that?

Jordan held Teresa back, knowing she was about to make the same mistake. Knowing if someone didn't stop her, she would either be taken too, or killed. He got her son taken; he wasn't going to be to blame for her too.

Jordan lowered his head into his hands, guilt and shame washing over him. "I'm so sorry," he croaked.

Teresa slapped him, hit his downturned head, kept hitting him until the palm of her hands were numb.

"It doesn't matter if you're sorry!" she yelled. "He's gone! He's fucking gone! Why would you stop me? That's my son!"

Teresa broke down. She fell forward into a heap on the ground, inconsolable.

She felt Tim's touch on her back, and she turned on him. "How could you have let this happen?" she asked, tears falling freely.

He said nothing.

"I trusted you," she whispered.

"We're going to get him back. I swear it."

James and Nate came out from hiding with Chong. They saw what had happened. "It doesn't matter," James said. "It doesn't matter who's fault it is. We have to find him."

"How are we supposed to do that? Do either of you have any iota of a clue as to where these people are headed?" Tim asked.

They were silent. Clueless.

"I do."

They all looked up at the stranger who stood looking grim.

"You're one of them?" Jordan asked, recognition dawning on him.

"I'm Officer Sanchez. I've been in deep cover for ten months. And I know where they're headed," Jose said.

"We need to get help," Teresa said. "There has to be police who can help, or the military. Who's your boss? Can you call in reinforcements?"

Jose shook his head. "I don't have the authority to do that. We can't blow this operation. And even if I did have the authority, access to this area is blocked. Rainier erupting really messed some shit up, if you haven't noticed."

"I have to get my son!" Teresa cried.

"And I'm going to help you do that. But you must understand I'm not even supposed to be talking to you. I could ruin everything by helping you. If we're going to do this, we're on our own."

"I don't understand," Tim said. "If you're undercover, then the police know about them, whoever they are. Why do they care if you go in there with guns blazing?"

"It's too soon. These people run a huge human trafficking operation. They're into some bad shit. We can't blow everything for one boy, as much as it pains me to say it." He looked at Teresa. "I need you to understand I'm going to do everything I can to help you and your son. I just can't call in the cavalry until I get the orders. Comms are still down. Until they're back up, we're on our own. Even when they *are* back up, there's a high probability we're on our own. Are you willing to accept that?"

Teresa nodded without thinking. "I'll do anything to get him back. Whatever it takes. I understand."

Jose looked at all the others, nodding their heads. "Alright then."

THEY UNLOADED THE TRUCKS AS FAST AS POSSIBLE, DRAGGING their captives to the blacked-out room in the barn. Gary watched with a grin on his face, pleased with the results of the mission. He thought of how proud he was of Rick, how loyal and competent he was. Then he realized he hadn't seen him yet.

As he took a closer look, Gary realized that his people weren't smiling like they should be, like they usually were. Morale is an important factor in any operation. Gary made sure his people were satisfied or they wouldn't put up with his abuse. No, something was wrong.

"Hey," he called out to no one in particular.

Everyone stopped what they were doing. It seemed they were on bated breath.

"Why is everyone so goddamn low? We won big, didn't we?"

No one answered.

A sliver of fear ran up his spine. "Where's Rick?" Gary asked.

Silence.

Gary raised his eyebrows. "I said, where is Rick?"

"He-he's not here," Kevin said.

"Where the hell is he?"

"He's dead."

"He's what?"

"D-dead, Gary. He got shot. By that kid who saved us from the rooftop in Puyallup."

Gary took out his gun and shot Kevin.

LUKE STUMBLED BEHIND THE OTHERS IN LINE. HE TRIED TO keep calm but the only thing he could think of was the look on his mom's face when she saw them taking him away. He hated himself for getting into a situation like this. "I shouldn't have followed Jordan," he whispered.

"Shut up," someone said, kicking ash up at him. The sudden intake of ash set Luke off into another coughing fit. He doubled over, barely able to catch his breath. His eyes watered as he struggled to breathe.

"What the hell did you do to him?" a woman said.

"Nothing! I just told him to shut up."

"You know Gary doesn't want damaged goods."

"It's not like we did a fucking health screen before we grabbed them."

"Don't be a smart-ass." The woman patted Luke on his back, trying to help him. It didn't do anything but sting.

"I'm fine," Luke choked out.

"Good, then let's keep going," she said, nudging him forward.

GARY SAT ON THE FRONT PORCH SMOKING HIS VICTORY CIGAR, listening to the creak of his rocking chair as he thought about the events of the day. He scoffed, thinking about shooting Kevin. "That little shit was always on my nerves anyway," he said to himself, justifying his actions.

He looked down at the blood splatter that was still on his shirt. He hadn't wanted to waste any water trying to get it off, so he left it there. It was a good reminder to his people, anyway. It's what happened when bad news was delivered.

Gary thought about Rick and the warning he'd given about Felicity before they left. "I wonder..." Gary said to himself, considering the possibility that she was the true cause of Rick's death. He realized he hadn't seen Felicity around the place either, and it really got him curious. But then why wouldn't Kevin have just said that? "Fucking Kevin!" he ground out.

Gary blew out a puff of smoke into the night air, both frustrated with his people, and satisfied at the amount of product they had managed to get their hands on. He looked up into the sky, taking note that there was no more ash falling. "Won't be long now," he said.

The sound of tires on the gravel driveway grabbed his

attention. Gary's eyes drifted to see a car rolling in slowly. "Now who in the hell do we have here?" he wondered aloud. He didn't have to give an order, his people were already on it, greeting the newcomer.

The driver of the vehicle parked in the middle of the driveway, instead of pulling all the way up, and the head-lights were still on, blocking his view of whoever it was. Gary gave them a minute to sort things out. Several figures started heading toward the barn.

"Who is it?" Gary called.

"It's me, boss," Jose answered. "I brought some goodies with me."

LUKE SHIVERED, PACKED IN NEXT TO A BUNCH OF OTHER people who he couldn't see. The room he was in stunk like human waste. Most were crying. Everyone, even those who weren't, was too afraid to speak. He hugged himself, shiv-ering against the chill.

"Where you been, Jose?" Luke heard people talking outside the door.

"Got left behind trying to grab these here." Something thudded.

"Damn boy, good for you."

The door cracked open, blinding Luke and the others with the lights from inside the barn. Luke was knocked back when something hard hit him. The door shut again, sending them back into darkness.

"Luke? Luke, are you here?" a voice whispered.

"Mom? Is that you?"

He didn't have to go far to find her. She was right next to

him, had been thrown into him when they locked her in. Teresa latched onto him, crying.

"Oh my God, Luke," she cried into his shoulder. "I'm never letting you out of my sight again," she said between breaths. "Are you okay?"

Luke held her just as tightly. "I'm fine. I'm so sorry, Mom."

"It's not your fault. Don't ever think any of this was your fault."

"How did they get you? I thought you were with—"

"With us?" James said.

"James! Oh my God, no."

"Shh. We have to be quiet," James said. "It's okay, man."

"What do you mean, it's okay?" Luke asked. "How can it possibly be okay?"

"We have a plan," came a whisper so faint Luke wasn't sure he'd heard right.

"Who's that?" Luke asked.

"Shh," James said again.

Question after question ran through Luke's mind. How was his mom here with James? And who was this other person? Where was Tim? And most importantly, what was the plan?

JORDAN AND TIM STOOD IN THE SHADOWS, WAITING FOR THE signal. "Do you think we can really trust him?" Jordan asked in a whisper.

"We don't have much of a choice at this point." Tim looked up at the sky.

Jordan looked up too. "No more ash falling."

"There's still going to be smoke for a long time. The lava started a forest fire."

"Who knows when they'll be able to put it out."

"Exactly. You have the keys?"

Jordan jiggled them in his pocket. "Yep, right here." Chong wiggled around at the sound.

"I can't believe you brought the dog with you."

"What else was I supposed to do with him?"

"I don't know. Anything." Tim threw up his arms. "You could've left him in the kennels with the other dogs. They were all safe enough."

"He was my mom's. He's not getting left anywhere but with me."

Tim didn't respond. He wasn't in the mood to argue, although he could've easily pointed out how quick Jordan had been to leave the dog behind when it came to getting his revenge earlier.

"Do you think there are people who—you know."

"What?" Tim asked.

"Are trapped. I mean, I know basically, the whole south Puget Sound is stuck, but I mean, do you think there are any trapped by the lava?"

Tim frowned. "I'm sure there are. I'm sure there are a lot." He thought again about how he should be out helping as many as he could. He'd been in such a hurry to get to the US Geological Survey, now he was having regrets. Tim wondered if the military really was out there helping trapped survivors and how many they'd be able to save.

"I recognize you, you know," Jordan said. "From the news. You tried to warn us."

"I didn't do enough."

"But it was better than anything anyone else did."

"It wasn't enough," Tim said again. He clenched his fists, furious at the situation. "I could've done something else.

Anything to save more people. People like this"—he waved his arms around—"shouldn't be able to take advantage of a situation like this. If we would've been more prepared—"

"Don't blame yourself," Jordan said. "You tried. You're still trying, even now."

CHAPTER
FORTY-TWO

Something is off here, was the first thing that ran through Gary's mind. He watched Jose closely. Nothing *looked* off. But after years in his line of business, Gary learned to trust his gut. "Tell me again how you managed to grab three individuals all by yourself?" he said once Jose was back from the barn.

Jose smiled, hiding the fear behind his eyes. "It wasn't by myself. When the raid was happening and everyone was freaking out, the two kids were an easy catch. They were tied up already, and I had the woman in hand when everyone started leaving. I was too far away from the group, I guess. No one heard me yelling for them to wait. So, I was forced to finish up by myself."

Gary's lips turned into a thin line.

"By all accounts, you disappeared."

Jose shrugged. "Everyone was busy. It was a cluster."

"Where's Felicity?"

Jose shrugged. "Dead."

Gary arched an eyebrow. "You're acting pretty casual about that. Weren't you two a thing?"

"Yeah, we had our fun. But business comes first. And she was clingy as hell, asked too many questions too."

"Uh-huh. So, what happened?"

"Kevin shot her."

Gary gave a slow nod, thinking it must've been Rick's way of handling their little rat problem. "I'd like to see these individuals you managed to grab."

"Sure thing, boss."

Jose led the way to the barn.

THEY STOOD TOGETHER IN SILENCE FOR WHAT FELT LIKE eternity, waiting for Jose's signal. The walkie-talkie finally went off. "Hey boys, Gary and I are taking a walk back down there. Have everything nice and pretty for him, please," came Jose's voice through the speaker.

"There's our signal," Tim whispered.

"Wait," Jordan said. "What if something goes wrong? What do we do then?"

Tim shrugged. "We'll have to make it up as we go. Hope for the best."

"I lost both of my parents." Jordan cleared his throat. "During all of this fucked-up insanity, I lost both of them. Not from *Rainier*," he sneered, "from stupid *people*. I don't know if I can handle seeing any more good people getting hurt. I don't know how I'm going to live with myself after all this is over, as it is."

"I hope no one else gets hurt either," Tim said. "I'm so sorry for your loss and I'm sorry to have to ask you to be a part of this, but we need all the help we can get. It's just us and we don't have any more time. It's now or never. Are you with me?"

Jordan thought for a moment then nodded.

"Good man. Let's go."

They stayed in the shadows, creeping around to the back side of the barn, where the back entrance was. The lights from inside the barn shone from beneath the door. They stood next to the generator. "Are you ready for this?" Tim asked. Once they started, there was no going back.

Jordan nodded. "Do it."

Voices were outside the door. *This is it*, Teresa thought. She held on to Luke and Nate with all the strength she had. James was holding on to Luke too. They were together. They were ready.

They shielded their eyes against the blinding light when the door opened. "The last ones who were brought here, step forward," a voice called.

Teresa stepped forward, blocking the boys with her body.

"Well, well, well," a man said, a smile in his voice.

His voice sounded familiar. Teresa tried to clear her vision so she could see who he was, but she was still disoriented from the sudden light. *Keep your eyes closed*, she reminded herself, squeezing them shut again.

"Good job, Jose, my friend. Well done," the man said.

"I'm glad you're pleased, boss."

"More than pleased. Jose, do you realize who you've just brought to me? This is literally the one woman I wanted to get my hands on. I never thought I'd see her again. You, my friend, have earned yourself an enormous bonus for this."

No, no, no! Teresa thought, recognizing the man's voice. *Not him!*

"Thanks, Gary!" Jose said, playing his part.

"What about us?" one of the other men in the barn asked. "We helped bring her in."

Gary laughed. "No, you didn't. But you know what? I'm in such a good fucking mood now, thanks to Jose here, I'll give everyone a bonus! How about that?"

Cheers went around.

Then the lights went out.

The sound of retreating steps came. "One of you check the generator," Gary said. "I'll keep this one with me." He reached for Teresa, who was only an arm's length away.

Teresa's eyes flew open. She could see, now that it was dark again, but she didn't need to see in order to know who the man was. The one in the truck, who tried to kidnap her. "Now!" she screamed, pushing forward, bringing the boys with her. The entire room of people behind her pushed forward as a collective unit.

Gary was knocked off balance. When he threw out his arms to try catching himself, he gut punched James. Teresa heard his "oomph," but didn't have time to stop and check if he was ok. She pulled the boys past Gary's flailing arms, past the men who were yelling, disoriented now that they were in the dark.

"Shut the door!" Gary yelled.

"Where are they?" someone cried.

"Shoot them!"

"Don't shoot, you idiot!"

"Run!" one of the captives cried.

The captives continued pushing their way past Gary, who was still disoriented. Some kicked at him, trying to get even a piece of satisfaction out of his pain. Most of them were too afraid to do anything but run. They just wanted out.

GARY PULLED OUT HIS GUN AND SHOT. HE AIMED WHERE HE thought most of the captives were and shot five times rapid fire. "The next one to move gets shot. If I see *any* movement from anyone, your ass is next!" he yelled.

No one dared to move.

"Boss?" Jose said. "What do you want me to do?"

"Get the fucking lights back on," Gary growled.

TERESA FELT THE DRAFT OF COLD AIR ON HER FACE. THEY WERE so close to the back door. Escape was within reach. Her heart lurched with Gary's gunshots. She lay on the floor with the boys, listening to their heavy breathing. "It's ok," she breathed in a whisper. "We're almost there."

"I'm scared," Luke whispered back.

She kissed his hand. "I know, baby."

Someone was walking toward them. A cold sweat broke out on Teresa's forehead. She could see, but only well enough to make out a man's form, not which man it was. It could be Jose. Or it could be Gary.

Her grip on Luke tightened.

"Wait a minute." Gary's voice came from farther away. "You see anyone over there, by the door?"

Adrenaline surged through Teresa. It was Jose next to them. They'd be able to get out. Without waiting, she pulled the boys with her, inching forward slowly. Jose would be able to see them, but she knew it was too dark for Gary and the others who were closer to the front of the barn.

"Yeah, there's someone over here. You want me to shoot?"

Teresa's eyes went wide. It wasn't Jose. It was someone else. And he saw them.

CHAPTER
FORTY-THREE

Jordan stood in the doorway next to Tim, watching everything. The only thing *not* going according to plan, was the boss of the operation shooting in the dark. They'd been counting on him not wanting to kill anyone because then he'd be losing money, or at the very least not wanting to hit his own people. They'd been wrong.

"She's moving," Jordan whispered.

"I know," Tim said.

"What do we do? He's going to see her."

"Too late, I think."

The man walking through the barn saw Teresa and the boys the moment they moved. Jordan and Tim had about five seconds to do something.

"Start the generator," Tim breathed.

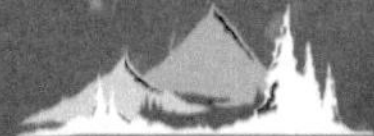

Something was moving against his leg. He looked down. Through his front pocket, he saw the glowing light of his phone. The phones were back. And he had a message.

THE LIGHTS CAME BACK ON, BLINDING EVERYONE. A GUNSHOT rang out, and then another. "Run!" someone yelled. Teresa wasn't sure who but didn't care. She was pulling the boys up with her as fast as she could. Everyone else started running too, heading for the front of the barn.

Teresa started for the back, where Tim and Jordan would be waiting. A hand grabbed her. "No!" she cried out, trying to pull away but the grip on her arm was too strong.

"Shut up, bitch," Gary growled in her ear.

"Mom!" Luke yelled.

Teresa let go of him, not wanting to drag him and the others down with her. "Go!" she yelled.

Gary was dragging her away, one hand around her arm, another locked into her hair. She was stuck. "Time for a little payback for earlier," he said, yanking her head back when she wasn't walking fast enough to the front. "Where's your nosy friend to save you now?"

"I'm right here, asshole!" Tim yelled.

Gary spun around, laughing. "Of course you would be here. And how did you find this place? Was it Felicity?"

"It doesn't matter," Jordan said. "You're not going to hurt her."

Gary arched an eyebrow. "Oh, I'm not?"

"No," Jordan continued. "If you do, you have no leverage. So you're not going to touch her." He took a step forward.

Gary laughed. "No leverage? I have a farm full of my

people right outside, friend. I don't need leverage. I have everything I want." He took a step toward the barn door.

"Let her go." Jose stepped toward Gary, pointing a gun. "You're under arrest, Gary. Time to let her go."

Gary shook his head. "And here Rick and I thought Felicity was the rat. Never pegged you for it. Shame on me." He pulled Teresa away again.

"Gary, stop!" Jose yelled.

"You're not going to shoot me." He kept walking.

"Let her go, Gary!"

"No one is going to come any closer, or her brains are going to go flying. Do I make myself clear?"

Tim looked at Jose with pleading eyes. Jose didn't notice. He was watching Teresa.

STILL HALF-BLINDED BY THE LIGHT, TERESA WATCHED THE figures of the boys huddled down in one of the barn stalls grow farther away as the man pulled her to the front doors. She looked to Jordan with wild eyes, hoping he would understand that nothing could happen to them. No matter what happened, *nothing* could happen to her boy.

She stumbled and he yanked her back again. Her eyebrows furrowed. There was something hard in her pocket. She couldn't for the life of her think what she would have in her pocket. Then she remembered.

Slowly, so the man wouldn't notice, she reached her hand down and grabbed Nate's pocketknife. The cold air hit her as she took her first step out of the barn. She looked at Jordan and mouthed, "Please."

Gripping the pocketknife with all her strength, she plunged the knife backward into the man's stomach.

"Fuck!" he cried. His grip loosened from shock and pain, and it was all Teresa needed to get away.

THERE WERE LIGHTS EVERYWHERE. THEY WEREN'T ALONE, after all. Police in uniforms and bulletproof vests flooded the yard, helping the captives who were still running away and arresting Gary's employees. Teresa ran back toward the barn and red dots appeared on Gary's chest.

Gary cried out, dropping to his knees, throwing one arm up and holding the other against his injured stomach.

"Wait!" came an unexpected cry from a little voice. "That's my dad!" Nate came running forward, arms reaching for his dad.

Gary looked just as shocked as everyone else. He watched his son run to him. "Nate, what are you doing here? I thought you were on a field trip—" It hit him then, where his son was supposed to be. The color drained from his face.

"Nate, get back here!" Jose called. "Gary, hands up."

"I'm bleeding—"

"I said both fucking hands up, now!"

Gary raised both hands as Jose and the other officers moved in. "Don't do anything stupid while my kid is here, Jose."

"That depends entirely on you, boss."

Nate reached his dad, tears streaming down his face. He latched onto him, hugging him as tight as he could. "I knew it was you," he said. "I knew it at the helicopter."

"Why didn't you say something sooner? I had no idea you were here." Gary scowled. "Were you in the barn with them?"

"You promised you didn't hurt anyone. You said that wasn't what your business was about."

"Son—"

"I had to see for myself."

Gary clenched his teeth. "Nate, you have no idea what I've done for our family. You will never know—"

"Time to go, boss," Jose said. He pulled Gary's hands down behind his back and cuffed him before other officers took him away.

"Wait!" Gary demanded, but he was ignored, no longer the man in charge.

"Come with me, Nate. We'll get you taken care of." An officer took Nate's hand and led him away.

TIM EXHALED. "I'M SO GLAD THIS IS FINALLY OVER," HE SAID, referring not just to this place but to the whole natural disaster. If the phones were back up, it was likely they found a way to clear the roads. They weren't cut off anymore and supplies and help would get through.

"You and me both," Jordan said.

They shook hands. Luke and Teresa were still holding on to each other, afraid to be apart for even a minute. The police were helping the captives, searching the property, and interviewing everyone else. For a moment, Tim looked into the sky and wondered about all the people who had to survive the past couple of days. "It all could've gone so differently," he said, shaking his head.

"If they just would've listened…" Tim thought about Joe

and Michelle, his bosses—former bosses—he didn't even know what they were anymore. Neither one had wanted to alert anyone about the eruption. He wondered if they'd be the ones fired now.

"I'll only drive myself crazy thinking about it." The only thing that mattered was that he helped as many people as he could, and he was going to continue doing so.

"I think it's time for us to get the hell out of here," Jordan said.

"I think you're right." Tim smiled.

TERESA SMILED DOWN AT HER SON, LOVING THAT HE HADN'T been too embarrassed to let her hold him in front of everyone. "I'm so proud of you," she said. "I want you to tell me everything."

"I will. But for now, can we go home?"

"Home might be underwater, but we can sure try."

Luke looked toward James. "Can he come with us? His family isn't here."

Teresa smiled. "Of course he can."

They walked hand in hand back down the driveway. They were finally together. Everything was going to be ok.

CHAPTER
FORTY-FOUR

Six Months Later

Tim smiled at the receptionist, wondering if she recognized him. Her icy glare told him that she did. "She's busy," she said.

"Somehow, she's always busy when I come around." He chuckled. "Sadly, I don't need your permission to see her." Tim continued past her desk to Michelle's office, stopping to knock as a courtesy.

"I'll call security!" the receptionist called after him.

"Go right ahead, dear."

Tim swung open the door to Michelle's office before she could answer. She turned from her computer with tired eyes, looking ten years older than when he'd last seen her. "Can I help you?" she asked, glancing from Tim to his companion.

Tim imagined himself standing in the same spot six months prior, desperate for her help. He saw her in a new light now that he knew the truth. "I just wanted to watch," he said.

"Watch what?"

"Jose, I'll let you handle this." Tim took a step back, giving

Jose plenty of room to walk around to Michelle's side of the desk.

"Michelle, I'm placing you under arrest. I came up here with Tim as a courtesy to you, to not cause a scene in the workplace. You can come willingly, or you can make things uglier than they have to be."

Michelle's eyebrows arched nearly to her hairline. "Arrested? Good God, for what?" she whispered.

Tim turned around the picture frame on her desk so that he could see the photo. He grimaced, holding it up to her. "For helping your husband in his human trafficking opera-tion. Don't act like you didn't know this was coming." He shook his head. "Poor Nate."

She lunged from her chair, reaching for Tim. "Don't you say his name!" she cried as Jose pulled her back.

"Don't blame me. *You* did this."

"Don't worry, he's going to be taken care of," Jose said. "Now I'm going to let you know what your rights are," he said as he handcuffed her.

TIM CLIMBED INTO HIS WAITING TRUCK. HE KNEW HE WAS doing the right thing; he didn't have a moment's doubt, but it was still going to take some getting used to. "Are you okay?" he asked Nate.

"Yeah."

"You don't have to watch."

"I told you I wanted to. I need to see Jose putting her in that car."

The guilt threatened to overwhelm Tim as he watched Nate's last parent getting taken away from him. All he could think about was losing his own parents and how it had felt. He never wanted to be the cause of such pain to anyone, especially not Nate. Tim sighed. "I'm so sorry, kid."

Nate scowled. "Don't ever be sorry for what they did. You didn't do this." He looked back out the window to watch his mother get into the back of Jose's squad car.

"Why didn't you tell us? All that time together and I had no idea."

"I didn't want you to look at me differently."

Tim was silent. He wanted to think that Nate was wrong. He wouldn't have viewed Nate any differently because of the actions of his parents. He told himself it didn't matter now, anyway. It was over. When Jose drove away, Tim shifted to reverse.

"Let's go home," Nate said.

Tim smiled, liking the sound of that.

THANK YOU

THANK YOU FOR READING!

Enjoyed Rainier? Please consider leaving a review.

Reviews help authors more than you might think. Even just a few words make a difference and are greatly appreciated. You never know if your words might inspire the next reader to pick up this story!

ACKNOWLEDGMENTS

Mount Rainier is close to my home and heart; I see it on a daily basis (if the clouds aren't blocking my view). Living in such proximity to an active volcano, an author can't help but wonder, *What if...*

After learning about the Oso Landslide in Washington state, I was inspired to write the prologue of this book. I encourage you to look up the devastating real-life events that took place there in 2014.

I'd like to thank my husband and son for everything they have done and continue to do to support me. Thank you for every moment you've been there, watching me learn and grow as an author, for every encouraging word, for listening to every complaint even when you don't understand what I'm talking about. Every milestone, big or small, you've cheered me on. Thank you for believing in me and thank you for giving me the most amazing life, the one I grew up dreaming of. I'm so blessed to have both of you. I love you to infinity and beyond.

To my mom, thank you for being the first to read my book, and thank you for always believing in and supporting me.

To my editor and proofreader at My Brother's Editor, thank you for helping me take my vision and make it shine. You are both invaluable to the writing process, and I am so fortunate to have found you.

Finally, last but certainly not least, thank you, dear reader, for showing your support in my writing by reading this book. Whether you are new to my work or are coming back for more, I truly hope you enjoyed the read.

ALSO BY K. LUCAS

Inferno Road

Arachnophobia

You Kill Me

Lost

Our Little Secret: A Novella

I Am Not OK

The Neighbors

The Wrong Stranger

ABOUT
K. LUCAS

K. Lucas is an author who lives for the unexpected twist. Originally from California, she now lives in the Pacific Northwest with her husband, son, three dogs, cat, chickens, and ducks. After earning a bachelor's degree in information technology, she became a homeschool mom and then a full-time author. She loves all things thrilling & chilling, and her favorite pastimes include reading, watching scary movies, and exploring nature.

To subscribe for text message updates
text KLUCAS to 877-618-4214

Website:
www.klucasauthor.com

Sign up for updates:
www.klucasauthor.com/newslettersignup

amazon.com/author/klucas
goodreads.com/klucas
instagram.com/author_klucas
facebook.com/author.klucas
twitter.com/AuthorKLucas
tiktok.com/@klucasauthor
pinterest.com/klucasauthor
bookbub.com/authors/k-lucas